What Could Go Wrong?

A Bailey Fish Adventure

Auntie Linda

Linda Salisbury

Tabby House

Cover by: MarionDesigns
Author photo: Jim Salisbury
Photo: James Mercer Langston (page 147),
Oberlin College Archives
Additional photo credits appear in the
acknowledgments.

ISBN-13: 978-1-881539-71-1
e-version: 978-1881539-72-8

Library of Congress Control Number: 2016906037

Manufactured within CPSIA guidelines.
Digital Impressions Inc.

June 2016 Batch 1

baileyfish@gmail.com
www.lindasalisburyauthor.com
Facebook: Author Linda Salisbury

Classroom quantities and *Teacher's Guides* available.

Tabby House
P.O. Box 544, Mineral, VA 23117
tabbyhouse@gmail.com

Contents

1
Where's Molly?

Bang! Thud! Then a shriek from the baby a few seats ahead who hadn't stopped fussing since they had left Florida. The plane from Fort Lauderdale to Costa Rica that Bailey and her grandmother, Sugar, had boarded just two hours earlier, shivered and bounced in turbulence.

Five minutes ago the pilot had asked passengers to take their seats and fasten their seat belts because the ride might be bumpy. Bailey hadn't realized just how bumpy it was going to be! The plane went up and down and sideways. A child's blue backpack fell from an overhead compartment and a woman screamed when it hit her shoulder.

Bailey grabbed Sugar's hand and closed her eyes. *I hope we don't crash*, she thought. *I want to see Mom in Costa Rica. Nothing is supposed to go wrong on our vacation, even if we're only on the trip because Mom's marrying Bug Man.*

The plane's bumpiness reminded Bailey of the crazy roller-coaster ride she had tried at Busch Gardens, except she always knew that the scary loops would end soon. Now she wasn't so sure. She gripped Sugar's hand harder. *Make it stop!* she thought. She buried her face against Sugar's shoulder. *Just stop bumping!*

"Everything will be okay, dear heart," said Sugar. "We'll be fine." Sugar always seemed to know when Bailey was worried, and Bailey *was* a worrier.

Twenty minutes after the plane had entered the bad weather, it was safely through it. The captain's soothing voice apologized for the moments of rough conditions. He said, "Now you can enjoy the rest of your ride. We'll be landing soon. The temperature is 80 degrees."

"See," said Sugar, "we've made it."

Bailey peered out the small window as the plane taxied to the gate at the Juan Santa Marie International Airport in San José. She had had a good view of the mountains beyond when the plane circled before landing. Although she had brought a history book to read on the three-hour flight, she hadn't opened it. Instead, Bailey had looked out the window because she wanted to see what she could of Florida from the air, then the beautiful blue-green Gulf of Mexico and occasional puffy clouds.

She and Sugar had driven in the dark for a 6:30 A.M. flight from Richmond, Virginia, to Fort Lauderdale. They then had to wait until noon for the plane to San José where her mother, Molly, would meet them. Bailey sighed. She couldn't wait to see her mother, but would have preferred that the trip was just a trip, not for them to be part of Molly's wedding.

Sugar leaned toward Bailey as the plane neared the terminal so that she could look outside, too. "Here we are. A new adventure. We'll go through immigration and customs, and then we'll find your mom."

"Immigration? Customs?" asked Bailey, unbuckling her seat belt.

"Every country wants to know who is coming in and what they are bringing with them. We'll show our passports and tell them that we don't have fruit or vegetables—or other things we shouldn't have," said Sugar.

Bailey and her grandmother walked through the terminal with their small suitcases on rollers, showed their passports, answered a few questions, such as the reason for their visit to Costa Rica and how long they planned to stay, then walked outside into the hot air.

"Wow! This feels like Florida in the winter, but not Virginia!" exclaimed Bailey. She looked around. "I don't see Mom anywhere."

Sugar said, "Let's wait here in the shade. She knows when we were supposed to arrive."

Bailey tucked her medium-length brown hair behind her ears and searched the crowd for her mother's face, then reached for her camera in her backpack. While she waited she could take pictures of palm trees and people. Her first picture was of a younger girl named Cora, who was holding a camera in front of her face. Cora reminded Bailey of herself at that age—shy but curious.

Bailey listened to passengers calling out to family or friends. "Hola, Stella!" "Hola, Pepé!"

She wished she knew more Spanish rather than just "hello" and "please." She decided that when she saw her mother, with her thick dark wavy hair and big sunglasses, she'd shout, "Hola, Mom!" just to surprise her. But where was Molly? It seemed like everyone who had been on their plane had been picked up or had boarded small buses to take them to their hotels.

Sugar looked at her wristwatch.

"Do you think Mom's forgotten that we're coming?" Bailey asked.

"Never. I suspect that traffic might be bad," said Sugar. "Molly's had to come through the mountains, and from what she's told me, the roads are narrow. Sometimes you have to stop for herds of goats, sheep or cows wandering along."

Bailey wasn't convinced. "Couldn't she call?"

"My cell phone doesn't seem to work well here," said Sugar. "There's a bench. Let's have a seat. We can still spot her when she pulls up."

Bailey dragged her suitcase to the wooden bench and plopped down. She closed her eyes for a moment and wondered what was going on at home at Lake Anna. Her dog Goldie was probably wandering around the house looking for her. Her cats, Shadow and Sallie, would be sleeping on her bed. Her friends, Noah, Fred, and Sparrow, were probably finishing up homeschool for the day and would go out to feed their horses and check on Goldie. Justin would also stop by to feed her pets. And they all would look after her grandmother's bookstore. Sugar's Book Barn would be closed for the week while Sugar and Bailey were away, but packages might be left at the front door. The boys would take them inside.

Bailey already missed being home, even though it was only 10 degrees when they got in

Sugar's pickup that morning for their ride to the airport.

Sugar rummaged through her purse and rustled papers, then said, "Wait here with the suitcases, Bailey, while I go back inside to see if someone can call your mother's cell phone number for me. I'll just be a minute."

Bailey watched Sugar briskly walk away as another group of excited passengers and family barged out the doors. They were smiling and laughing and passing a small boy they called Pepito from one grown-up to another, smothering him in kisses.

Lucky Pepito, thought Bailey. The boy's family squeezed into a taxi van and sped off. Bailey waved good-bye to Cora when her family loaded their car with suitcases and left for home.

Bailey looked at her watch and twisted a strand of her hair.

Another car pulled up and stopped with its caution lights blinking. The driver, wearing a chauffeur's cap, reflective sunglasses, dark jacket and pants, got out and walked to the sidewalk where Bailey was sitting with one leg draped over her suitcase. The driver raised a sign on a stick that read: BAILEY AND SUGAR.

Bailey and Sugar? "I'm Bailey. Just a minute while I get my grandmother," Bailey said excitedly to the driver. "But wait, I can't leave my suitcases. Can you go inside with the sign? My grandmother isn't very tall, and she's wearing brown slacks and a blue plaid shirt and she's looking for a phone."

The driver nodded, said nothing, and took big steps while carrying the sign through the terminal doors.

2

A welcome surprise

Bailey wondered if she had done the right thing. Maybe the driver would get lost in the airport and never find Sugar and then what? Should she have left the suitcases with the driver and looked for Sugar herself? No, she might have gotten lost, too.

She wheeled both suitcases closer to the doors that were constantly opening and closing with people heading for buses and taxies or friends picking them up.

Then she saw Sugar returning and just behind her was the driver holding up the sign.

"Sugar, look back!" Bailey pointed when her grandmother was near the door. Sugar glanced over her shoulder but evidently didn't notice the driver. Bailey was about to say it again but just then the driver tapped Sugar on the shoulder and showed her the sign.

"I'm so glad someone has come for us," said Sugar. "We were getting worried."

"Hola!" said the driver with a voice that was deep but sounded strangely familiar. "I told you there might be goats on the road."

Bailey's hazel eyes widened. "Do you know my mom? She said there might be goats."

"Better than you think," said the driver, removing the cap. Long dark wavy hair cascaded below the driver's shoulders.

"Mom!" shrieked Bailey, forgetting that she had been worried and even a little annoyed while they waited and waited.

"Well, I'll be," said Sugar with a huge smile.

"I wanted to surprise you, and I guess I did. Sorry I was late. I had to wait for two herds this time, one of goats and the other of cows up in the hills before I could get on the highway,"

Cows wander in the road.

said Molly. "The cows refused to be hurried even when I honked and took their picture. Now give me hugs and let's get the bags in the car before I get a ticket."

"What a funny disguise, Mom," said Bailey. "We didn't know it was you." She slid into the back seat.

Molly turned and grinned. "You didn't really think I'd forget my matron of honor and best girl, now do you? So, how was your flight?"

"Really bouncy, but Sugar said we'd be fine," answered Bailey. Her mother didn't seem to be listening. Molly eased the car through the airport traffic and onto the busy highway. She never stopped talking as she pointed out shops and restaurants that she liked.

Bailey studied the countryside during the short ride to Heredia, which Molly said means city of flowers. She was amazed that the trees and plants looked so much like Florida's.

"After we leave the main road," said Molly, "we'll stop at my favorite *soda* where they cook outside—sodas are what the *Ticos* call the little roadside restaurants, sometimes like food trucks. We'll have a refreshing fruit drink. Then, depending on which animals decide to use the road, we should be at Hacienda Marie in less than an hour."

"What's a Tico?" asked Bailey. She was always curious about new words.

"That's what the Costa Ricans call themselves," Molly replied. "And another term for you to learn while you are here is *pura vida*. That means pure or good life and also good-bye and lots of other things. We are full of beautiful life in Costa Rica," Molly said.

After they turned onto an even bumpier road, they slowed to follow sheep and a shepherd in no hurry.

"Hola!" shouted Molly as they passed the flock. "I always say hello to sheep and goats in the road, and their shepherds."

Bailey sees an oxcart in the middle of the road.

Molly waved as they drove on.

Bailey tried to take a picture with her new camera of a small cart pulled by oxen. She hoped the picture wouldn't be blurry from the car's motion as they passed it.

A Tico cooks outside the family soda.

Little sisters let Bailey take their picture.

16

The little lunch place consisted of a small building painted yellow with green trim and a dirt parking area. On the left side were a few colorful plastic tables and chairs and a taller wooden table where food was cooking in electric pots. Two boys, about Sparrow's age, were sitting nearby on steps and twin sisters waved at Bailey from their small chairs. Bailey took pictures of them and the food area.

The owner, who was cooking, spoke to Molly in Spanish. Then Molly told Bailey that even though they were only stopping for fruit drinks, he wanted Bailey to sample his special *gallo pinto*. "You pronounce it gai-yo," said Molly.

"What's that?" Bailey asked as the man scooped a small amount of food into a red plastic bowl and gave it to her with a spoon. He smiled and nodded, waiting for her reaction. He handed a similar bowl to Sugar.

Bailey looked at the unfamiliar dark rice and beans mixture. She wasn't sure about this, but Sugar was smiling and saying, "Delicious. I'd love to make this at home."

The cook said, "It's simple. You cook the rice, you cook the beans, then you cook them together and add your spices."

Bailey took a small bite and then another. "It's really good," she said, surprising herself.

"Come back again," said the soda's owner.

"I'd like to," Bailey said. "Then I'll eat a big helping of 'gai-yo' pinto. Did I say that right?"

Molly gave her a hug. "You bet. That's my girl."

The hilly road narrowed even more and Molly shifted gears several times before they reached a more level area. Molly seemed to know that Bailey would be hungry about now, and reached into her large bag and pulled out three bananas.

"These are very local—from Marie's yard," she said.

"They're bigger than the bananas we grew in Florida," said Bailey. "Remember how tiny those were?" She peeled back the yellow skin.

"And you and your friends didn't want to eat them because they didn't come with a label from the store," Molly said with a laugh.

The sweet fruit brought a flash of sadness as Bailey thought about the house where she and her mother had lived in Florida before her Molly sent her to stay with Sugar.

"There's the hacienda—my friend Marie's house. She owns the coffee plantation here and runs it herself. With help, of course." Molly honked and waved at a gardener wearing a floppy straw hat.

"That's her uncle Chico," Molly said. She stopped the car under a tall kapok tree. Just beyond was a large adobe house with wide shady porches. Paddle fans slowly moved the air above the green wicker rocking chairs near the front door.

Bailey opened the car door just as a woman, with dark hair, much like her mother's, came out of the two-story house with a metal roof.

"Hola! Welcome to mi casa, my hacienda, my house," called Marie. "Come in. Uncle Chico will help you with your bags."

3

First walk about

Bailey waited quietly while Molly made the introductions and Marie hugged Sugar. It was hot. Bailey wished that she could just go to her room and change into shorts and flip-flops even though the shade and gentle breeze were refreshing.

"Oh, and this is my wonderful daughter, Bailey," Molly said, grabbing her around the waist.

"I've heard so much about you," said Marie reaching out her arms. "Let's go inside. My aunt Lupa is a wonderful cook and she's prepared coconut flan and a papaya drink for you. You've already met her husband, Chico. They practically raised me after my mother died and my father worked long days on the plantation."

Marie's warm smile made Bailey feel very welcome.

She remembered that her mother had told her that flan was a delicious custard served with syrup. It sounded really good after the long day of travel.

"First I will take you to your rooms," said Marie.

Bailey followed the grown-ups into the house and up the polished wooden steps to her small room that overlooked the hills covered with coffee trees. "I'll show you how we grow the beans and make them into coffee," said Marie.

Bailey's bedspread was the color of orange sherbet and there were photographs on the walls of someone, maybe Marie, when she was Bailey's age, patting a dog, or holding a kitten, reading a book in a hammock, or riding a pony. A small desk and chair were near the window, and there was a white wooden dresser with three drawers next to the closet.

Sugar's bigger room was next and then Molly's. Her many clothes for parties and the wedding were neatly hung everywhere.

"After our snacks, we'll take a walk," Molly said. "I want to show you where the wedding will be. Then Andrew and his boys will be here tonight when we have a party with our friends."

Bailey felt the old gloomy feeling settling on her like a smoke from a campfire that stung her eyes. She tried to remember how kind and generous Dr. Andrew Snorge-Swinson, whom she called Bug Man, and her mother had been. Just before Christmas, they had made it possible for Bailey's friend Justin and his family to stay in their home instead of having to move when their landlord decided to sell it.

However, that was before Christmas, and this was now, just a week later. And her mother was actually getting married on New Year's Day. Her life with her mother would never be the same.

Bailey hung up her long lilac-colored dress in the closet and changed into her denim shorts and blue T-shirt. She placed her favorite Lake Anna hooded sweatshirt on her dresser. It would probably be too hot to wear it unless they went up into the mountains.

Bailey unpacked her book bag and placed her library book, the one for her school report, on the table next to the bed. It was about plantation life in the South before and after the Civil War. Because Hacienda Marie was on a plantation, Bailey decided to ask Marie about plantations in Costa Rica to see if they were like the ones she had been reading about in Virginia and other Southern states.

The window in her corner room was open to let the warm breeze catch in the paddles of the slow-moving fan. Bailey leaned out the window. She could see Chico back at work in the garden, cutting flowers with long stems. He placed them gently in a woven basket. Bailey noticed a little black cat watching him from beneath his wheelbarrow. Was it friendly or shy? She needed a pet friend at the moment, someone she could share her secret gloom with. She missed Shadow and Sallie and dear Goldie. Pets always seemed to understand and they never said, "You shouldn't feel that way."

Bailey jumped when she heard a loud knock. "C'mon, girlfriend," her mother called. "Snack time, and then we'll take the walking tour."

Bailey called, "Coming," and slid her suitcase under the bed.

Her mother had changed out of the taxi-driver suit and was wearing bright lemony Capri pants and a loose white blouse with long sleeves that she had rolled up above her wrists. Her thick hair was tied up with a soft green scarf. Her large sunglasses were perched on top of her head.

Lupa's flan.

Bailey eased into a kitchen chair and Lupa handed her a small dish with the mound of custard, topped with lots of shaved

23

coconut over brown syrup. She looked at her mother's face as Molly sat down across from her. She was more beautiful and happy than Bailey could remember. For a moment Bailey thought it was because they were finally together again, but then Molly said, "Coconut flan is a favorite of Andrew's. We fix it for him all the time."

It's always all about Bug Man. Bailey put her spoon down without taking a bite, but when she looked at Sugar's face, she knew it was the wrong thing to do. She poked at the flan, tasted a sliver, and had to agree that it was delicious. She happily finished it, even if it was Bug Man's favorite dessert.

The walk took them first around the house, then to the garden. Chico was no longer there but the fuzzy black cat was sleeping. Bailey bent down to stroke her fur. Marie said, "If you pat Belleza, which means beautiful, she will be your friend for life. She'll want to sleep with you since you are staying in her favorite room."

Bailey grinned. "I love cats. That would be great!"

Belleza stretched and yawned, then got to her feet to follow Bailey, Sugar, Molly, and Marie.

Marie led them through the hillside where the coffee beans were growing on small trees.

Coffee grows on the hillsides of Marie's plantation.

Each coffee cherry, or seed, contains one or two beans that are later roasted.

She picked the red beans called "coffee cherries" and said that the coffee beans were only brown after they were roasted.

"Really," said Sugar. "I thought they were picked when they were brown, like nuts."

Marie laughed. "Hardly. There are a lot of stages to growing coffee and getting it to your kitchen, Sugar. We do things the old-fashioned way here. We harvest or pick the cherries by hand, rather than machine, then dry them in the sun. Look over there and you'll see them. We have plenty of rain here so we use what is called the 'wet' method of processing the beans. We put them in fermentation tanks to get rid of outer layers, then the beans are dried and most are packaged in sacks for export."

Sugar said, "I had no idea it's so complicated."

"That's not all," said Marie. She pointed to the sacks of beans that workers were carrying into a storage shed. We sell most of our coffee beans to big companies but we always roast some for ourselves. Trust me, it's the best."

Bailey looked at Sugar. "Maybe I could write about this for school," she said, "because I have to learn about plantations, crops and the people who run them. Coffee would count."

Sugar nodded. "Good idea. We can come back later this week with your camera and a notepad."

Marie said, "I'll be happy to answer all your questions, Bailey. We have coffee samples for you to take home. But first, I want you to taste our special brew."

She led them into a room where Chico had poured small cups of coffee, including one for

Bailey. The room was fragrant with the odor of freshly brewed coffee.

"Just a little taste," said Marie. "You don't have to finish it."

Bailey took a small sip. It was stronger than the flavor of coffee ice cream, but not bad. A small sip was all she wanted, though. Molly and Sugar finished their samples and held out their cups for more.

"And now we'll go to the wedding site," said Marie. "It's just a short walk."

"It's such a beautiful place," Molly whispered to Bailey. "You'll see."

4

More gloom

Bailey wished she had worn sneakers instead of flip-flops as they walked down the stony hill through the coffee plantation. Marie suddenly turned to the left and a few yards ahead was a clearing surrounded by many colors of flowering hibiscus. Some of the flowers were as big as dessert plates. At the edge of the wide clearing perched a simple gazebo covered with vines. Molly was the first to reach it. She stood in the center with her arms outstretched. "Look at this view!" she exclaimed. "Isn't this magnificent!"

The clearing.

The rolling hillsides below were dotted with fields of tropical fruits and flowers surrounded by rows of palm trees. In the distance Bailey could see a meadow filled with a herd of grazing goats. The mountain breeze rustled in the palms. There were no traffic fumes and no people. It was as pretty as Molly had told them.

"We'll have a rehearsal, of course," said Molly. "During the wedding our guests will sit in chairs that we'll set up back there. Bailey, Sugar and I will walk in from over there, through that little arbor that I've draped with a light fabric and paper wedding bells. We'll add fresh flowers that morning. Andrew and his sons will be standing here, waiting for us, by the gazebo. Then, we'll have a tent back there for the reception. Marie has taken care of everything for us."

It was getting real. The wedding was going to happen. Bailey looked at Sugar. Her grandmother was smiling. Sugar put an arm around Molly's shoulders. "I hope this all makes you happy," she said. "It's been a long time."

A long time? What did Sugar mean? Wasn't her mom happy when it was just the two of them in Florida? That was almost a year ago, but not a long time. Bailey's gloom deepened, but she knew she had to keep it to herself.

The arbor that the bride, her matron of honor, and best girl will walk through.

She turned away so that her mother wouldn't see her face. Bailey was startled when a sudden movement rustled leaves underneath a pink hibiscus bush. Then she realized that Belleza had followed them all the way and was stalking a green lizard. Bailey bent down to pat the little cat. "I hope you sleep with me tonight," she whispered.

Molly continued, "I think you'll like the music that I've chosen. Jorge—he lives way over by the beach—has a great voice and plays the guitar very well. He has a couple of friends who will join him. One plays a wooden flute and another the mandolin. They've composed original music and will play old favorites. You'll love it."

Bailey quietly pronounced "Hor-hey" for Jorge, just like her mother had done.

Sugar said, "This is splendid. Now, it's been a long day. I think I'd like to rest a bit, maybe on the porch, before everyone comes for the party."

Bailey wasn't in the mood for a party, but a rest would be good. She followed Sugar, Marie, and Molly back to the house, only half hearing the conversation. Little tidbits, like "Andrew," "his boys," "Bailey," and "soon."

When they reached the hacienda, Sugar quickly settled into one of the rocking chairs.

"Almost like home," she said. "Bailey and I like to rock in our chairs when the weather's good."

Molly blew a kiss and headed into the house with Marie.

Bailey plopped into the rocker next to her grandmother. *This is nice but I wish I were home*, she thought.

Sugar sighed from exhaustion. "What a long day, but I'm glad we made it."

Sugar rested her feet on a small stool placed her glasses on a glass-top table. After running her hands through her short, dyed- brown hair, she folded them in her lap and leaned back. As Sugar relaxed, her mouth settled into a smile, the kind of smile that made people smile back, even strangers.

Bailey thought about how Sugar was everybody's friend, but she was always willing to stand up for what was right.

I love her so much, thought Bailey. *I hope nothing bad ever happens to her.*

Sugar's eyes soon closed and she was sleep-breathing.

A moment later, Bailey's eyes closed, too.

5

Not ready to party

When Sugar's snoring woke her up, Bailey realized that the sun was lower in the sky, and sweet Belleza had found her lap. The screen door opened and Molly bustled out. Sugar blinked her eyes and yawned.

Molly said, "I'm glad you two caught up on sleep because the party will start in about thirty minutes. I can't wait for you to meet more of my friends and Andrew's sons—your new brothers, well, your stepbrothers, Bailey."

Bailey buried her face against Belleza's neck. She decided not to ask her mom anything about Bug Man's boys. She was sure she wouldn't like them. They would look like their father, Dr. Andrew Snorge-Swinson, with similar ponytails and thick glasses, and they'd probably be allergic to dogs and cats like he was. Well, there was no way she was going to give up Belleza for them during the time she would spend at the hacienda! It was bad enough when

Bug Man had visited them in Virginia and sneezed all the time.

She felt her grandmother's hand on hers.

"Bailey and I'll go get ready," said Sugar.

When they were upstairs by themselves, Sugar hugged her and said, "Dear heart, I know you have mixed feelings about all of this."

Bailey nodded.

"Me, too," Sugar confessed. "But this visit is for your mother's wedding, and we need to try to make it a good time for her."

"I know," said Bailey.

"I'm sort of curious about Andrew's family," Sugar continued. "Sometimes I even imagine his sons looking just like him. Miniature Snorge-Swinsons."

Bailey snorted. "Me, too." She grinned.

"Who knows, we may both be surprised," Sugar said. "Kids aren't always like their parents, by the way they look, behave or believe."

Bailey thought of how different she sometimes was from the mother she loved. Bailey looked more like her father, Paul Fish, with his hazel eyes and faint freckles on his nose, and she was shy, not at all like Molly who always seemed to be the life of the party. But she and her mother loved each other and had had a lot of good times, especially when they lived in

Florida together. That was before Molly took her dream job and went to Costa Rica and promised to come back to live together in Florida. Staying with Sugar had been wonderful, especially after Bailey had gotten to know people in her neighborhood and at her new school. Sugar was kind and caring, and always listened.

However, she had never expected her mother to stay in Costa Rica instead of coming back to the United States. And she hadn't expected her mother to fall in love with Bug Man, the man she had written articles and then a book about. And she hadn't thought her mother would actually marry him!

"And one more thing. I already have the feeling that I won't be able to spend as much time with just you as I thought. Your mom wants me to help with errands and to visit with her. I hope you don't mind, but I know you'll be fine during those occasional times. Just let me know if you need anything," Sugar said.

Bailey said, "I'll be fine." She didn't feel entirely fine about it, but she'd work things out. Besides, she had reading to do.

"Ready to go down?" asked Sugar.

"I guess," said Bailey. She took a quick look in the mirror and smoothed her hair with her fingers.

6

Meeting Bug Man's boys

Bailey paused on the landing halfway down the stairs as she tried to spot her mother in the rooms filled with people she didn't know. Then, she heard Molly's voice from out on the verandah saying, "I can't wait for you to meet my sweet Bailey and my mother, Sugar!"

The door opened and Molly came inside, followed by Bug Man and his sons. Bailey squinted for a better look just as Dr. Andrew Snorge-Swinson noticed her on the stairs.

"Hello there, Bailey," he called. "Come on down." He sounded really happy to see her, like they were old friends.

Bailey didn't let go of the railing as she slowly went down the last few steps. The crowd of Molly's friends parted and she saw Bug Man smiling and holding out both hands as if he wanted to give her a hug. Bailey knew her mother expected her to let him and so she did, but without hugging back, at least not hard. He turned her around so that she could see his sons. She was amazed. Neither had a ponytail nor glasses. Both boys were well-tanned. The taller one had a mop of shiny dark hair that came to below his ears, and the other had short, wavy, light-brown hair, almost the color of hers.

"Meet, Fendol—Fen we call him," Bug Man said as he turned to the shorter boy with the lighter hair. The boy's brown eyes studied Bailey with a serious look. "And my older son is Archer—Archie. Family names." Archie's even darker eyes didn't smile while he stared at Bailey. It wasn't a glare, but it wasn't welcoming. She felt uneasy.

"Nice to meet you," said Bailey. She wasn't sure if she should hold out her hand to shake theirs, but decided against it.

The boys mumbled the same, still staring, then they smiled as if it was expected of them, but she knew they didn't mean it.

"Now that you kids have met, why don't you go outside and get acquainted since we're all family now. Well, after you get some snacks," said Molly cheerfully. "Yummy shrimp and lots of goodies over there in the dining room."

Molly made it seem like they were in preschool and were told to be nice and go play. Bailey didn't feel much like family and it seemed weird to have to go talk to these strangers, even though they were about her age. But, she and Sugar were doing everything during this visit for her mother, and Bailey knew her grandmother was watching. So, Fendol, Archie, and Bailey filled up their plates with dips, cheese, crackers and fat pink shrimp and went outside.

The night air was still warm. There were strange screechy sounds in the trees, which Bailey later learned were often made at sunset by howler monkeys. The boys sprawled in green wicker chairs that were away from the main door and Bailey rocked and nibbled her snacks. She couldn't think of anything to talk about. It was "awkward," as her half sister, Norma Jean, would say.

Finally Archie said, "So, how d'ya like Costa Rica so far?" He tilted his head back and popped a plump shrimp in his mouth.

"I dunno. We just got here," said Bailey, adding, "and we won't be staying long. Just a few days. Then Sugar and I are going home."

"I know. You live in Virginia," said Archie. "Dad said he visited you a couple of times there and told us all about you and your animals and especially that you didn't like him much."

Fen coughed and kicked his brother.

"Ow!" said Archie. "But it's true. He said that he heard that you even called him 'Bug Man.' Pretty mean of you, I think."

Bailey was shocked that their father knew how she felt and that he had even told his sons.

"Well, I like him better now," she blurted. "It was just . . ."

"That's okay," said Fen, with an edge to his voice. "We weren't happy about him falling in love with your mom, either. She isn't anything like our mom. We call her . . ."

"My mom's a wonderful person," Bailey interrupted loudly. "Don't say anything bad about her." Her hands gripped the arms of the rocker.

"Well, so's ours," said Fen. "Or was. After they got divorced Mom moved to Idaho and then died in a boating accident."

Bailey gulped. "I'm sorry. That's terrible."

"It *was* a terrible accident. But we've had our dad all to ourselves for the last six years and we like it that way. But now," Fen continued. He glanced at his brother. Neither said anything for a few minutes. Bailey wished she hadn't come outside with them. She didn't want them to be in her life, wedding or no wedding.

Fen gave Bailey a sideways look and said, "Look, I don't know how you feel, Bailey, but it sounds like you don't like the idea of them getting married either. We want to see the wedding stopped before it's too late."

"We have some ideas," said Archie. "We think they'll work."

"What?" She sat forward quickly and her plate tipped off her lap, spilling shrimp and dip to the floor. She stopped rocking. Her mind was spinning. "But how would you do that? I mean, the wedding's all planned."

"That's why we need your help," said Archie.

"What?" her face flushed. "I . . ."

"We'll let you know when the time comes what we need you to do. Now, swear you won't say anything," said Fen, "or it won't be good."

7

Mixed feelings

Bailey stared at the dark sky splattered with faint stars. She couldn't think of anything to say. Yes, she'd be very happy if her mother and Bug Man didn't marry and Molly came back home for good. Molly would then move into Sugar's house at Lake Anna and they'd all live together. Only, she knew that Molly wouldn't enjoy living in an old house in the woods where it snowed sometimes. She might want to travel again and write other books or articles about someone else.

On the other hand, Fendol and Archie didn't think that the marriage was a good idea for their dad and themselves, and they knew their father, Bug Man, better than Bailey did. But how could kids stop the wedding? It was going to happen in just a few days. Wouldn't the grown-ups get mad if they found out?

And why didn't Archie and Fendol like Molly, or was it just that nobody could replace their mother? Or was there something else? She didn't want to know what name they called her mother. It couldn't be nice.

"Why don't you like my mom?" she finally decided to ask.

The boys looked at each other. "That's our business," said Fen.

"But the big part is that we like to spend time alone with Dad," Archie said. "We go with him into the rain forest and into the estuaries when he's collecting specimens. It was great until your mother started going along, or alone with him when we were visiting."

"Visiting?" asked Bailey, confused.

"Yeah, we've been in boarding school in California this past year, while *they* were working on *her* book. We haven't spent much time with him," Fen said.

"Oh," said Bailey. "I didn't know." She hadn't seen much of her mother either since Molly had met Bug Man. But as much as she wanted her mother to herself again, did it make it right to try to stop the wedding?

"So will you help us?" asked Fen. "Now that you know something's going to happen, you'll be blamed anyway so you might as well help."

Bailey's head was pounding. She didn't know what to say. The party was getting noisier. She could hear her mother and Sugar laughing. The music was louder and louder and so were the adults talking.

"Well," said Archie, "since you haven't said *no*, it must be a *yes*. Are you ready to hear our plan?"

"No. I need time to think," Bailey said. She was suddenly very tired. "I'm going inside."

Fen jumped up and blocked her. "Like I told you before, don't you dare say anything."

Bailey wiped up the spilled salsa with her napkin and shoved a shrimp toward Belleza.

Without looking back at Bug Man's sons, she opened the screen door and stepped into the crowd inside.

8

E-mail for Bailey

Bailey found Sugar talking with Marie and Lupa in the kitchen. She hugged her grandmother and buried her head in her side. "What's up?" Sugar asked. She lifted Bailey's chin so they could look into each other's eyes. "Something the matter? Shall we go outside and talk?"

Bailey so wanted to tell her grandmother about the boys, but she had to think about what they said first. What if it wasn't true? What if they were just trying to get her in trouble by having her tattle on them?

"I'm just tired," she said. "Do you think its okay for me to go to my room?"

"Sure," said Sugar, "but say good night to your mom and Andrew. I know they'll understand that it's been a long day."

"Have one of our lemon-coconut cookies first," said Lupa. "It's my own special recipe that I'll share with you. I was just going to take them into the buffet."

Bailey let the sweet tartness melt on her tongue and gladly accepted another when Lupa offered the plate again.

When she reached her bedroom Bailey saw that someone had hooked up a laptop for them to use on a small desk near the window. Bailey powered it on and watched her e-mail slowly load in.

The first was from her father.

From: <pjfish2005@yermail.net>
To: "Bailey"<baileyfish@gmail.com>
Sent: 4:15 p.m.
Subject: Hi

Hi Bailey. You're probably enjoying lovely warm weather in Costa Rica and we've been dealing here with ice. Just after you left, we had quite a storm. Freezing rain and high winds. Good thing your plane left Richmond before it got bad.

Justin's doing a good job of taking care of Goldie and the cats. I stopped by to see if he needed help because of the storm but he had already chopped away ice from the steps. We're hoping for warmer weather tomorrow.

We are all wondering if you arrived okay and how everything is going. Norma Jean wants you to take a lot of pictures.

Love, Dad

Bailey hit REPLY:

From: "Bailey"<baileyfish@gmail.com>
To: <pjfish2005@yermail.net>
Sent: 9:58 p.m.
Subject: Hi back

Hi Dad. The plane ride was fine but bumpy and Mom met us at the airport and tried to trick us with a disguise. Marie's house is big and I have a room upstairs near Sugar's. We went to Marie's coffee plantation. I think we go to the beach soon and maybe we'll see Dr. Snorge-Swinson's research place where he studies bugs. Thanks for checking on Goldie and the cats. I really miss them and everyone. Tell Norma Jean I have lots and lots of pictures already. Here's one I took of some little boys named Ricardo and Manny and their pets, a kitten and a parrot. They let me hold them when we stopped for lunch. Their father was cooking outside. I have a picture of their sisters, too. Bailey

There was also an e-mail from the Keswicks. She had never had one from them before because they lived next door. It was easy to run across Sugar's backyard and through the woods any time she wanted to talk with brothers, Noah and Fred, and their little sister, Sparrow. They were her best friends, besides her Norma Jean, Emily, and Justin, who lived not far down the road. They told her how much they missed her and wanted to know if she was going to see a volcano. Sparrow asked if Bailey liked her new stepbrothers, and if they were fun like Noah and Fred.

Bailey never thought she would miss her Virginia friends so much, and she'd only been away part of a day. She was glad that her father had gone to see Goldie, her wonderful rescue Walker hound, and her cats.

That was enough for now. She tucked her hair behind her ears. With all the windows in the hacienda open wide for the night breeze, Bailey could still hear the laughter and loud talking from the party. The paddle fan above her head swirled slowly. Bailey turned off the desk light so she could get a better view of the yard and the stars before she climbed into bed. She saw Archie and Fendol walking quickly away from the house, down toward the field where the cars were parked. One of them was carrying a large stick. He was tossing it up in the air and catching it as it twirled back toward him.

Bailey was too tired to care what they might be up to.

9
Toucans

For a moment when she woke up Bailey thought she was home in her own bed with Shadow or Sallie purring on her pillow. A fuzzy cheek with tickly whiskers was pressed against her face. She reached around to pat the cat and realized it was Belleza. "You *are* beautiful," she said.

Bailey rolled over to look at the clock. It was seven A.M. Central Time. If she were home it would be eight A.M. and she would have already had finished her breakfast. Bailey rolled out of bed and quickly dressed. She glanced out the window, but no sign of Bug Man's sons. They were supposed to be staying with him somewhere else, but they sounded like they would be around in the morning. She wished she would never see them again.

Today she, Sugar, Molly, and maybe Marie, would be driving to Dr. Andrew Snorge-Swinson's research lab where they would see his insect specimens. He was very well-known for his studies of leaf-cutter ants. Bailey was interested in seeing these creatures march around carrying bits of leaves, but she'd rather spend time alone with her mother. She really hadn't had much of an opportunity for doing that in a long, long time.

Bailey found Lupa in the kitchen. She had cut up fresh pineapple, mango, papaya and bananas and had a plate of warm homemade muffins ready.

"Good morning, Bailey," said Lupa. "It's nice having someone your age in the house again. Someone who's up early and wants to see the toucans."

Bailey's eyes opened wide. "Toucans? Here? I didn't know I'd see some even though my mom e-mailed me a photograph once."

Lupa said, "There are many different kinds of toucans all over Costa Rica. Now, take your plate and go sit on that bench and watch for them. They come for the fruit. I always give some to the birds. Marie loved to spend time with them when she was little."

Bailey asked. "Are the pictures in my room of Marie?"

"Yes. She grew up here with her father, Pedro. My husband Chico, helped him run the farm in addition to teaching at the university where I also taught part time. The coffee plantation has been in the family from way back. Now Marie owns and runs it. She has a very good head for business," said Lupa. "Hurry. The toucans will be here."

This reminded Bailey of what she had learned about Clara Garland, a young woman, who with her sisters, had run plantations in Louisa County both before and after the Civil War. Clara was very brave, and wanted enslaved people to be free and educated. Bailey had also been reading about John Mercer Langston. He was the son of a white Louisa County plantation owner, who lived with Lucy Langston, his freed slave. She was American-Indian with black heritage. John had an amazing career and became a lawyer, gave speeches, and was elected a United States congressman.

What stories would Marie have to tell her about this plantation in Costa Rica? When Bailey sat on the bench that Lupa had pointed out, she noticed a bird feeder with an unusual shape hanging from a hook near the hacienda. It was carved from a fresh pineapple into the shape of a basket and contained pieces of melon and banana inside it. Colorful birds pecked at the fruit and butterflies swarmed around.

Awesome, thought Bailey. She grinned when two toucans strutted into the yard. Their colorful long beaks, almost as big as their bodies, reminded her of the brown pelicans that also had huge beaks.

Bailey is amazed by the brightly colored toucans that appear in Marie's yard.

The toucans ate pieces of fruit that Lupa had tossed on the ground earlier, then flew into the trees, where they hunted for insects and snakes, just as Lupa said they would.

Shortly after she had lost sight of them, Bailey heard her grandmother and mother talking in the kitchen. They would have enjoyed watching these birds.

Molly leaned out the window and called, "When you've finished breakfast, girlfriend, we'll be ready to go to Andrew's lab. Grab your camera."

Bailey wished she had had her camera with her when she was watching the birds. She'd have to remember to bring it down with her tomorrow. She planned to make an album of her trip photos when she got home so she wanted to make sure that she had pictures of all the wonderful birds she saw.

10

Bug center

Marie's Jeep bounced along the rough dirt roads through the countryside. They saw other plantations where farmers were growing bananas, coffee, melons, mangos and many kinds of palm trees, and workers' houses near the edges of fields. The bumpy roads took them up hills where Marie explained that they were at the edge of the rain forest, where it was wet much of the year. Different types of trees and

A worker's house on the side of a hill.

ferns grew there than on the rolling hills down below.

They passed the entrance to a chairlift through the forest's canopy. Molly said if they had time later in the week they might ride up in the little cars so they could see different birds and snakes, such as poisonous vipers. They were tiny, but dangerous, she told them.

As they drove, Marie turned on the windshield wipers. It was raining just a little. Finally, up ahead, Bailey could see a large wooden building with a tin roof and wide covered porches. A wooden sign at the driveway entrance read:

ANDREW SNORGE-SWINSON, PhD
FIELD RESEARCH STATION
ENTOMOLOGY

They had arrived. Marie parked in the least muddy section of the area near the steps to the door. Bailey had expected Bug Man to greet them, but she didn't see him anywhere.

Molly bounded ahead and went inside. Then she returned with a puzzled look.

"That's a surprise," she said. "Andrew said he'd be here by nine." She looked at her watch. "And it's already 9:45."

Sugar wiped the moisture off her glasses. "I'm sure he'll be along soon," she said.

"We can go on in," said Molly. "I've been here so many times that I could give the tour."

She turned on the lights and said she'd try to call Andrew. When he didn't answer, Molly texted him. There was still no response.

"Well, cell phone service isn't the best up here. Let's have a look around."

Molly led Sugar, Bailey, and Marie down a hallway with Bug Man's book-filled office on one side. On the other was a smaller office that she said was hers when she was writing about him. Bailey was happy to see photographs of herself next to her mother's computer. The main area was in a large room with windows covered with screens instead of glass. *I wonder if the screens keep the bugs in or out,* thought Bailey.

Shelves were filled with samples of different kinds of insects. It was like a museum filled with wings. In the center of the room was a large glass case with sticks and freshly cut leafy branches.

"Look closely, but don't lean on the glass," said Molly. "Those are the magnificent leaf-cutters at work! And there are forty-one species."

Bailey had to admit it was pretty amazing. Each of the ants in the line was marching while carrying a large section of a green leaf over its body. It looked as if the ants had umbrellas

Leaf-cutter ants with large pieces of leaves on their backs walk along a branch. Ants are specks in these pictures on this page.

Dark shapes are pieces of leaves carried by tiny ants.

above their backs. *How could something that small carry something so large?* she wondered.

"And look at this specimen of a

Close-up view of an ant carrying a leaf.

owl butterfly," said Molly, holding it up for Bailey to look at closely. "There are 1,500 species of butterflies in Costa Rica, and this is one of my favorites. Andrew has so many wonderful insects displayed here in his lab. People from all over the world come to see him and his collection."

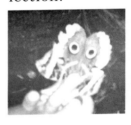

Molly shows Bailey large owl butterflies, called buho in Spanish.

Suddenly they heard screeching brakes and a car door slam. Bailey turned to face the doorway.

Dr. Andrew Snorge-Swinson pounded into the room. "Sorry, I'm late."

He gave Molly a kiss. "My car was damaged last night. I had to get it fixed. Looked like a big stick fell on it and cracked the windshield. It took a lot longer than I thought to get it replaced."

"Oh, dear," said Marie. "Did it happen during the party? You should have told us."

Dr. Andrew Snorge-Swinson said he thought so, but he had parked near a tree and didn't notice the crack until he reached home.

Bailey's heart raced. That was terrible. Should she say anything about seeing Fendol and Archie and the stick? She stuck her hands in her jeans pockets. It would be awful to accuse his sons if they weren't responsible, but what if they were? Was this part of Fendol and Archie's plan?

"Time to look around," said Dr. Snorge-Swinson, taking a deep breath and adjusting his thick glasses.

"Let me tell you about the amazing ants," Bug Man said to Bailey as they walked back to the glass case. "I suppose you think that the leaves are their food, but they eat a fungus from the bottom of the leaves. They can carry twenty times their body weight. They are just one of 4,000 species of insects found in Costa Rica, which is why I make my home and studies here. I'm always discovering something new."

Bailey took pictures of the ants carrying leaves up branches.

He pointed out other insect specimens that Bailey had never seen before, from giant spiders to a large beetle that was as big as a cracker. Bug Man told her about the variety of snakes in the country and the tiny colorful tree frogs that are poisonous. "Don't pick them up, even though they look harmless and pretty," he cautioned. "Native peoples have used the poison on the tips of darts or spears. No surprise that my boys are especially interested in learning about them," he added.

That's not good, Bailey thought.

"Look at these butterflies," said Molly. "So beautiful. Andrew has a butterfly house in the garden near his home. I enjoy being there in the morning when the butterflies are awake. They come and land on my finger, don't they, Andrew?" she said. He smiled and nodded.

"Now," said Bug Man, when he finished showing them around his research area, "we'll take a short walk through the rain forest. There's so much to observe if you look closely. Cover yourselves with this mosquito repellent, and no matter what you do, don't swat mosquitoes. It will make even more land on you. Just ignore them."

Bailey didn't like that idea at all, but she did as she was told. They walked through the dripping forest, with Bug Man pointing out the different types of trees, snakes, the tiny colorful frogs, and a huge termite nest that towered over all of them.

It was fascinating, but Bailey was glad when they reached the cars. Molly decided to ride with Andrew and the rest would follow them to a favorite roadside restaurant where they would have lunch. There was no mention of meeting up with Andrew's sons and Bailey didn't ask about them. She hoped they'd been sent back to boarding school.

11

What else could go wrong?

Molly told Sugar and Bailey that they'd be driving to the coast the next day to see a beach where the shells got up and walked around. When Sugar looked puzzled, Molly said that hermit crabs were living inside the shells and it was always a surprise to see them walking.

She said that first, on the way, Andrew wanted them to kayak or canoe through an estuary, where the river was slowly moving through a swampy area to the Pacific Ocean. Bailey knew exactly what an estuary was because when she lived in Florida, the Peace River was part of the Charlotte Harbor Estuary. She had studied how the estuary, a mix of salt and fresh waters, became a nursery for marine life.

"It will be a perfect day," said Molly. "Perfect. Perfect."

And it was.

Marie said she had errands to do so she'd meet them later for lunch at the beach.

"I know you'll enjoy the trip on the river, Bailey," said Molly. "I've done it several times and I always see something new. You can decide if you want to paddle a kayak or a canoe, but either way it's recommended that a guide rides with you."

As they parked in the shade at the boat rental shack, Bailey groaned to herself when she saw that Archie and Fendol were already waiting there with their father. Fendol smirked as he walked past her with a paddle.

Bailey pretended she didn't notice. She helped Sugar carry the lightweight green canoe with three seats to the water's edge and the two of them climbed in after they fastened their life jackets. José, their guide, sat behind them and said he would tell them when he needed help paddling. Otherwise, they should just enjoy looking around at everything. Bailey watched as the others selected their boats.

Bug Man and Molly laughed when they almost tipped over as they stepped into their canoe. It was wobbly as they settled in, but their guide, Rico, steadied it before he climbed in behind them. Their laughter made Archie scowl.

The boys insisted that they didn't need a guide for their kayak ride and when their father finally agreed, they selected one with just two seats. Fendol said, "We'll follow you guys. We'll be fine."

Bailey and Sugar's canoe was the first in line to head down the river. The branches of the mangroves reached across the water. They were like bony hands clasped together above them, creating a leafy tunnel.

Bailey was surprised at how similar many of the plants were to those she had seen in Florida when they took walks or boat rides on the Peace River. She noticed mangroves with leggy roots that disappeared into the water. It

Mangrove forests are found in tropical or subtropical areas. The stick-like prop roots look like legs. The roots are ideal as a nursery for young fish.

was almost like home. But she had never seen a sloth before, or snakes dangling from branches, or crocodiles sleeping on muddy banks. José pointed them out to Bailey's amazement. Then, she and Sugar were startled by a loud clapping noise and then another. José said that the sound was made by big clams, as they snapped closed.

Bailey could hear her mother talking quietly with Andrew and Rico behind them in the next canoe. She and Sugar enjoyed the overall silence, except for the parrots and macaws, and the water dripping off José's paddle. Bailey smiled at how peaceful the river ride was. It made her forget why they were in Costa Rica.

But suddenly there was loud *thump,* a huge *splash,* and her mother's shout of, "Help! A yellow snake!"

Rico yelled, "Sit still, lady, I'll get the snake off you!"

Molly screamed again, then, Andrew yelled, "Oh, no! We're tipping over!"

Bailey turned her head and saw her mother, Bug Man and Rico bobbing about in the river and trying to turn their canoe right-side up.

"Where's the snake? Get it away from me!" Molly yelled, look around in the water.

"It swam away by now," Rico said.

"We're coming!" shouted Bailey, as José turned their canoe around and he and Sugar paddled hard to help with the rescue.

The splashing and shouting woke up the crocodile they had passed only moments earlier. It slipped off the bank into the water and headed toward the canoe.

"Are you okay?" Bug Man called to Molly.

Crocodiles and caymans sun themselves on muddy banks of the river. This one turned around and slipped into the water.

"Very wet," said her mother. "How do we get back in the canoe?" She sounded worried. Her thick dark hair streamed behind her in the water as she grabbed onto her paddle.

Bug Man and Rico boosted Molly back into the canoe. She stayed on her knees trying to help the others. But as Bug Man tried to climb in, he slipped back under water. When he surfaced, his thick glasses were missing. He blinked as water dripped down his face and from his ponytail.

Rico offered to help look took for the glasses, and swam down. The river wasn't deep but the water was tea-colored, which made it hard to see the bottom.

"Oh, dear, Andrew," wailed Molly. "This is terrible."

Andrew swam below the canoe several times. Each time he surfaced, he sputtered, but was empty-handed.

Another splash, and Bailey looked around and saw that her mother had jumped back in the river to help hunt for his glasses.

Sugar said, "I'd like to help but I'm not sure I'd be able to get back into a canoe. I'd just make things worse." Sugar reached out and held onto the other canoe so that it would stay in one position.

Bailey saw that the first crocodile was now closer and another huge one had opened its mouth really wide before it slipped in the

The crocodile swims towards them.

water, too. Their eyes were above the water, but their bodies were mostly submerged.

"Help us!" Bailey shouted to Andrew's sons, who had paddled way ahead.

A second crocodile joins the chase.

But Archie and Fendol were not helping. They were laughing.

"Stop joking around and help!" yelled Bailey. "Go back and keep that crocodile away from them!"

"Yeah, sure. We know exactly how to do that. We'll shout, 'Go away, croc,'" said Archie.

"I'll just splash him," said Fendol. "Like this." He lifted his paddle and slapped the water. "Oooooh. I bet he's scared of us now." The boys kept paddling away.

The crocodiles quietly moved nearer.

"Watch out, Mom!" screamed Bailey. "The crocodiles are heading toward you and . . . and Rico and Andrew."

Sugar let go of the other canoe. "Let's go back," she said. She and José quickly paddled behind Molly's canoe so that they could try to drive away the crocs. The closest one's eyes poked out of the water as it silently moved nearer. "I'll smack it with my paddle," José said. "That will be a distraction while they look for the man's glasses and get back in the canoe."

Bailey wasn't happy about paddling closer to the huge reptiles, but somebody had to help her mother and Dr. Andrew Snorge-Swinson, especially when his sons weren't.

Sugar said, "We can do it. We'll all splash." The three of them yelled and splashed and blocked the crocodiles from getting closer.

Bailey turned and looked back at Bug Man, who was ready to dive down again.

He must be really worried about losing his glasses, she thought. She knew he couldn't see well without them.

She wondered why their canoe had tipped over. Had the boys caused that to happen? Had they thrown the snake at Molly or did it just fall out of a tree? The boys sure didn't seem to care. They were laughing when they passed everyone and continued on.

When it was clear that José, Bailey, and Sugar had been able to distract the crocodiles, José paddled them back to Molly's canoe, which still had water in it. Everyone was soaking wet and back on board, but they had given up looking for the glasses.

"I have an old pair I can wear," said Bug Man, "until I can get new ones made. Don't know if the new ones will come before the wedding, though." He rubbed his eyes and squeezed water from his ponytail.

"You'll be fine, my dear," said Molly. She blew him a kiss. "I'm just glad we are all right."

"This wasn't how I wanted today's adventure to be," he said, sounding worried.

"Now where did those boys go?" Dr. Andrew Snorge-Swinson asked, squinting. "We were all supposed to stay together. I guess I'll have to have a talk with them when the river reaches the ocean and we turn in our canoes. They'll be waiting for us. My boys never pass up a chance to eat lunch at Selina's Seafood Shack."

12

Taco surprise

The sandy beach with driftwood on the Pacific Ocean was exactly like Molly had described it. The hermit crabs, living in the abandoned shells of other sea creatures, rested on the sand, then walked around. Bailey had never seen anything like this. She had watched shells moving on the beaches at Sanibel, where she and her mother had enjoyed spending time together. However, the Florida creatures were in

A sandy beach where hermit crabs walk.

their own shells. She remembered the tiny colorful coquinas that wiggled back into the sand after being washed up by the waves, and the olives that seemed to be drawing hearts, or other designs in the wet sand.

Molly smeared sunscreen on Bailey and Sugar, then they waded and splashed in the ocean. While their father watched from the

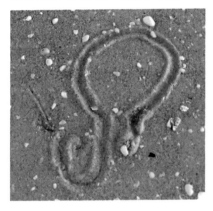

Bailey remembers the designs that the olives (an animal in a long, cylindrical shell) made in the wet sand on Sanibel Island.

Many olives are about two inches long. Their shells are a spotted sandy color, which helps them blend in with the beach. The creature that lives inside is like a snail.

beach, the boys raced ahead and kept their distance until it was time to leave. They all wiped sticky sand off their feet before driving to Selina's Seafood Shack for lunch. Molly said it was a popular place to eat for both locals and tourists.

Fendol and Archie quickly claimed a table by the window, a table with three chairs.

"Why don't you sit with the boys?" suggested Molly, cheerfully.

"I'd rather be with you," said Bailey, pulling out a chair at a table for six where the adults were about to sit down.

"Oh, go on," said Molly. "You kids need to get to know each other. You probably have a lot in common, beside me and Andrew." She gave Bailey a look that meant that there would be no further discussion. Bailey wished that Sugar would say something like, "Oh, Bailey should sit with us," but she didn't. Instead she was asking Andrew about how he became interested in the study of insects.

Bailey slouched as she joined the boys. She was annoyed that her mother was so clueless, and sorry that Sugar didn't notice how she felt either. Bailey moved the boys' backpacks, which they had placed on the third chair, to the floor. The chair's metal legs scraped on the sandy tiled floor when she pulled it away from the wooden table.

"Don't touch our stuff," whispered Fendol.

"Too late. I'm supposed to sit here," said Bailey.

"And you always do what you're told?" asked Archie so quietly that the adults couldn't hear. "We don't. Just when we feel like it." He looked over at his dad and gave him a thumbs up, and a grin, as if they were having lots of fun. Andrew squinted then smiled back.

Bailey studied the menu. She wasn't hungry anymore. These guys were bullies.

It was always hard to deal with bullies, whether they were boys, girls or grown-ups, and this was even harder because these bullies were Bug Man's sons. She thought about courageous people she had been learning about, from her great-great aunt Mae, a spy during World War I, and the other Wild Women in the family who were brave and adventurous, and always seemed to know what to do. Sugar was one of them, and Molly was too, at least the adventurous part. And from her readings she knew about John Mercer Langston and Clara Garland.

But what should she do about Archie and Fendol? She didn't want to know their plans.

She didn't want to be a part of their plans. Bailey didn't want to be around them. She would have to figure out a way to deal with them and not let them bother her. But standing up to people wasn't easy.

"Are you ready?"

"Huh?" said Bailey.

"To order," said the server. "You must be daydreaming, honey."

"Oh, sorry," said Bailey. She quickly scanned the menu. It was in Spanish.

Oh, no! she thought.

Fendol seemed to realize that she couldn't understand the words. He whispered to her with a helpful smile, "Why don't you have *pulpo*. We have it all the time."

Bailey wasn't sure what pulpo was, but she saw that the same word appeared under pictures of salads and tacos.

"I'll have a pulpo taco," she told the server, who quickly disappeared.

When the orders arrived, both boys had hamburgers and fries on their plates. Archie rubbed his hands together. "My favorite meal," he said. He squeezed catsup from a plastic bottle all over his burger and the fries.

Bailey looked at her taco. Little tentacles hung out of either end.

"What's this?" she asked the server when she returned to refill their water glasses.

"Problemo?" the woman asked.

"No problem, but I don't know what this is," Bailey responded, poking at the soft taco with her fork.

"Pulpo. Pulpo," said the server, who smiled, turned her back and headed for the kitchen. "Octopus."

The boys smirked as they watched the look of surprise on Bailey's face. She knew they expected her to complain or freak out.

Well, then, she thought, *I'll show them.*

She reached over for the sticky catsup bottle and squeezed it all over the octopus pieces in her taco, then took a big bite. The pulpo was chewy, but with catsup on it, didn't taste too bad. "Mmmm," said Bailey. "Yummy." She squeezed the catsup bottle again but aimed it in a different direction and red stuff squirted on Fen's hand, instead of on her taco.

"Oh, sorry," said Bailey. Her next squeeze splatted catsup on Archie's face giving him a red clown nose.

"Uh-oh. My aim isn't very good." She flashed a big smile and took another bite. This time the catsup squirted out of the end of her taco and it landed on the front of Fen's white shirt.

"Cut it out!" hissed Fen.

"It was just an accident," said Bailey. "Accidents happen." She looked hard at each of them, then gave them a knowing smile. "Like a snake just happening to *accidentally* land on someone in a canoe."

The boys looked at each other in alarm.

"So, *you* cut it out," said Bailey in a loud whisper. She was surprised at how bold she sounded, even though she was shaking inside.

13

Needed talk

Shortly after they returned to the hacienda, Sugar and Molly drove off to the local village. Bailey could have asked to tag along, but she felt that they wanted to be alone. She decided to spend time reading outside in a hammock. She wanted to learn more about Clara Garland for her school project that would be due three weeks after they returned.

Bailey was so focused that she didn't hear Marie walking over to visit with her. Perro, one of the plantation's little brown dogs was following her. Marie pulled a lawn chair next to the brightly colored hammock and said, "You are in my favorite reading spot. Now, my friend, what do you think about Costa Rica?"

Bailey said, "It's beautiful. It reminds me of Florida."

"I visited your mother in Florida before you were born," said Marie. "And I remember meeting your dad, too. How is he?"

"He's good. He and his new family live near us at Lake Anna," said Bailey.

"So I heard," said Marie. "I've only lived here on this plantation, except for when I went to college, then graduate school for degrees in agriculture and business. You have to know a lot these days to run a successful plantation."

"I'm reading about plantations right now—about people from long ago," said Bailey. "Do you mind answering my questions?"

"I'd be glad to," said Marie. "But first tell me about the people you are studying."

Bailey told Marie about John Mercer Langston and also Clara Garland.

"I see. Now for your questions," said Marie.

Bailey asked, "Are the plantations here the same as the ones that we have at home? Did your family have slaves way back in the old days?"

"Mmm. Good questions. I think the old plantations in both countries were alike in some ways and different in others," said Marie. "They are usually very big farms with large fields. We grow several crops here. We have the coffee beans, some sugar cane, pineapples and papaya, and a vegetable garden," said Marie.

"Your country used slaves for many years to work in the fields and houses," she added.

"The Spanish brought slaves with them to Costa Rica and sometimes stole them from the local Indian tribes, but by the early 1820s, slavery was abolished here and other Central American countries. So, yes, there are similarities, but I don't think it was as difficult to abolish slavery in Costa Rica or that we had as many problems with people getting along with each as your country did," Marie said.

Bailey said, "What about your family? Did any people in your family own slaves?"

Marie said, "To answer your most important question, my family came from a blend of different backgrounds, including Spanish, plus one of the groups of native people called Bribri. I have pictures of my relatives."

"However, my great-great-great grandfather married a freed slave, one of the Bribri, but my ancestors never owned slaves. Our workers, also from many backgrounds, have always been free. I'm glad."

"Wow!" said Bailey. "Some of it is like John Mercer Langtson's family."

Marie looked at her watch, then leaned forward. "Now, I have some things I've been wondering about," she said. "I hope you'll tell me while we have some time by ourselves. I hope you don't think I'm too nosy."

Bailey was startled. She didn't want to talk while she was lying down in the hammock, but as she tried to sit up, the hammock twisted like it was going to throw her to the ground. She rolled out of it and sat in the lawn chair next to Marie.

"Oops. That was awkward," Bailey said. "I haven't been a hammock much."

"Hammocks are like that," Marie said. "I've been tipped out several times myself." She paused then said, "Bailey, I have the feeling you are not happy about the wedding."

Bailey's cheeks flushed and she looked away.

"That's okay," said Marie. "People aren't always happy about the choices their parents or friends make."

Bailey nodded. *How can everyone tell how I feel?*

"But what I really need to know is what is going on between you and those boys of Andrew's. I watched what happened at the table in the restaurant. Before you answer, I want you to know that I think your aim with catsup is excellent." Maria leaned closer and smiled.

Bailey wasn't sure what to say. *Could Marie be trusted not to make things worse?*

"Let me tell you something else," continued Marie, without waiting for an answer. "Lupa and Chico have been worried that those boys are up to something. They've heard them talking and Chico saw them heading with a stick to where the cars were parked the other night. No matter what we think about Molly and Andrew's choice to be married, I don't think anyone has the right to destroy their plans. Do you agree?"

Bailey nodded.

"I really need you to tell me what's been going on because I can't believe you are a part of it," said Marie with urgency in her voice.

Bailey looked into Marie's brown eyes. They were so filled with care and concern that they reminded Bailey of how Sugar looked when they talked together about something important.

"Okay, I'll tell you," Bailey said, taking a deep breath and looking up at a palm tree. And then, all the comments the boys had made to her, and her worries about what might happen to spoil the wedding, and even how scared she was of Fendol and Archie spilled out. It was like when her cat knocked over a carton of milk and the milk splashed all over the counter and onto the floor. To her surprise, Bailey couldn't stop talking.

She hesitated for a moment and then confessed how she had called Dr. Andrew Snorge-

Swinson "Bug Man," and that made Marie smile.

Marie said, "Funny you should say that. His students at the university call him that, too, but because they like him, not to make fun of him."

Bailey's face reddened. "It wasn't because I liked him," she said. "Mostly I just thought it. I was mad that my mother liked him so much and she wasn't coming home." She twisted her hair.

"Please continue," said Marie.

Bailey still didn't feel better after she had told Marie, whose face looked puzzled, then serious, about the boys' mother drowning and why they didn't want the wedding to happen. Bailey told her that she really didn't know what they were going to do, or if they would stop now that she had squirted the catsup and told them to "cut it out."

Marie grabbed Bailey's hands. "I'm so glad you shared all of this. You don't need to deal with them by yourself. Pretend we haven't talked, and I'll handle things. Chico and Lupa will help look out for you," Marie said. "But, Bailey, if you are ever mad at me, I hope you don't have a squeeze bottle of catsup nearby. I usually wear white!"

Bailey laughed.

14

Time alone

Bailey watched Marie stroll back to the hacienda with the dog sniffing the grass behind her. Marie stopped to pluck a pink-and-white-striped hibiscus flower and waved at Chico in the garden before she went inside.

Bailey picked up her book. She didn't feel like reading anymore. Instead, she thought it would be fun to take a walk before Sugar and Molly returned from shopping. She placed her book on her chair and tried to decide which way to explore.

Hibiscus

Up the hill from the hacienda were more fields of coffee trees. To the right, were even more, and that was the way to the buildings where the coffee berries were brought for sorting. Behind the house was the area thick with trees where the toucans lived. The dirt road to town, which led down to pastures filled with goats, was behind where she stood. She decided to visit the goats. They reminded her of Gruff, the Keswicks' pet goat.

She was startled when something brushed against her leg, but when she looked down, she saw that it was Belleza.

"Want to walk with me?" she asked the little cat, and was pleased when she followed her, although Belleza dashed in and out of the bushes and up a tree instead of walking next to her. *Just like Shadow and Sallie*, thought Bailey.

The air was steamy in the afternoon sun, reminding her again of Florida, or even a few humid days in Virginia last summer.

After she reached the end of the long driveway from the hacienda, the road turned to dirt with deep ruts made by heavy rains. She walked carefully around them, often sticking to the edge where there were yellow flowers like the wild tickseed daisies that blossomed along Virginia country roads in August.

Several of the goats were near the fence when she reached their field. Three were curious enough to walk up and stick their whiskered faces through the fencing. But they were too shy to be touched. Bailey yanked a handful of grass from the roadside and was pleased when the youngest goat took it from her hand. The little brown-and-white kid waited by the fence, hoping for another treat. When Bailey gave him a handful, he let her pat his rough and bumpy forehead. The goats scampered off when they heard a car coming.

Bailey turned and saw that it was Andrew and the boys. Bug Man slowed and rolled down his windows and asked if she wanted a ride. She shook her head no, then called out, "Thanks, anyway."

The boys had blank looks on their faces as they stared at her from the car windows. She didn't know what that meant. The car continued toward the hacienda.

Bailey leaned against the fence and watched the goats again. Little ones were frolicking and climbing on rocks. Lupa had told her that her family milked the goats they owned and that she and Chico often made cheese. She planned to serve some at the wedding feast. "It's very good," said Lupa.

The wedding feast. Now that she had talked to Marie, Bailey knew she didn't want anything to stop the wedding, not unless her mom and Andrew decided to call it off on their own.

15

Missing

Belleza was way ahead of her when Bailey walked back to the hacienda, stopping to look at butterflies resting on orange flowers. She could hear another car, and when it tooted its horn, she saw that it was Molly and Sugar.

"Climb aboard the wedding express!" shouted her mother.

Bailey slid into the back seat filled with packages and shopping bags.

"Just wait till you see what we found. Lots of clever little gifts to give our friends," said Molly.

"I thought you would be the one getting the gifts," said Bailey.

"Everyone will have a souvenir of our happy day," said Molly. "Nothing fancy, but fun. As you can see, presents have arrived at the post office and we had a little shopping to do."

"What have you been up to, Bailey?" asked Sugar.

Bailey said that she had been reading her book for school, and then had walked to see the goats. She wondered if she should tell them about talking with Marie, but decided not to. They would have questions and she didn't want to say anything else at the moment. She decided to change the subject.

"Did you get anything for me?" It was something she always asked her mother when she was little and they didn't have much money. Molly always had the same silly answer: "Yes, sweetheart, an invisible pony." But with everything that had happened since they lived together in Florida, would her mother remember the game?

But Molly quickly answered: "Just what you always wanted, sweetheart. An invisible pony— your favorite color. It's a little frisky, though, so be careful."

She remembers, thought Bailey. She grinned. "I'll be careful, Mom."

When they reached the hacienda Bailey helped her mother and Sugar carry the packages and bags into the front hall, and then she went out to collect her library book.

The lawn chairs were still where she and Marie had been sitting with Perro, but her book was . . . was . . . missing.

"Huh!" Bailey looked around the lawn, beyond the hammock, then in the ferns and bromeliads along the edge of the trees.

Where could it be? Could it have blown off the chair in the breeze or did Perro snatch it? Bailey saw Chico with his wheelbarrow. Perhaps he would know. She ran across the lawn and tapped him on the arm. "Mr. Chico, my book is missing. The one I was reading in the hammock."

He turned to her and said, "Sorry, I haven't seen it, Miss Bailey. Maybe those boys know where it is. They were outside tossing a Frisbee for a while. I think they went inside."

Archie and Fendol. Of course. *Why hadn't she thought of that?* Bailey marched to the house, glaring. She wasn't going to bother saying anything about this to Marie. She'd deal with it on her own.

Just then her mother pushed through the door and said, "Bailey, I need you to help me find something. My wedding ring for Andrew is missing. Were you in my room while we were in town? I don't mean that you would have taken it, I just wonder if you saw anything." She sounded frantic.

Bailey said, "Not me. But my library book is missing, too."

Molly didn't seem to be listening at all. She said, "The ring has been in a little box on my dresser. I know it was there this morning. But it wasn't there when Sugar and I went upstairs a few minutes ago to wrap all these little gifts. Help me look, Bailey. We've got to find it."

Bailey decided that locating her mother's ring was probably more important than finding her book at the moment. *Would the boys have done that too? Would they be that stupid? Or was it part of their plot to stop the wedding? That would definitely be stupid.*

Molly's room was a mess, not like she usually kept it at home in Florida. At home all her clothes had been folded neatly and stacked in drawers or carefully hung in her closet. Her bed was made every day, and she expected Bailey to be just as tidy.

Now, her clothes were thrown everywhere, spilling out of her large suitcase, hanging out of dresser drawers, scattered on the bed as if a tornado had come through this room.

"Wow! Who did this?" asked Bailey.

"I'm afraid I made the mess," said her mother, tossing purple sandals out of her way. "I tore everything apart looking for that ring."

"Did you look behind the dresser?" Bailey asked.

"Yes, and under the bed."

"What about in the trash?"

"I wouldn't have put it the trash," said Molly, pulling clothes off the rack in the closet.

Bailey decided to look anyway.

She reached down in the small basket, which was filled with store tags from clothing, plus sales receipts, and her fingers felt a small box. She pulled it out. "Is this it?" she asked with surprise.

Molly hurried over, took the gray box and opened it. "Yes. Yes. The ring. But how did it get there? I'm sure I left it on the other side of my dresser. Oh my gosh, it could have been thrown out."

Molly grabbed Bailey and smothered her with a hug. "Oh, girlfriend, how can I ever thank you for finding it? Our wedding would be ruined without the ring."

"How about giving me an invisible pony?" said Bailey with a smile. She was enjoying every moment in her mother's embrace and didn't want it to ever end.

16

Accusations

Bailey hoped that finding the book would be as easy as finding the ring. She helped her mother straighten up her room and select tan slacks and a blue-and-while polka-dot blouse for dinner, before she searched again.

Bailey looked through the drawers and even the wastebasket in her room. No book.

All right, then, she thought. *Time to find Archie and Fendol. They think I'm a coward, but not anymore. What they are doing is wrong, wrong, wrong.*

Fendol and Archie were not hard to locate. Bailey heard them in the kitchen talking with Lupa. They were trying to convince her to give them more cookies before dinner.

"Just one more," Lupa finally said. "Then don't tease me about it again." Lupa saw Bailey coming in the door. "And some cookies for you, too," she said. "I know it's getting close to supper time, but when we have so many visitors and such a happy occasion, it's Lupa's Rules all the time."

"Thanks," said Bailey. She gave the boys a hard look. "I've something we can do together before supper. We can look for my book."

"Your book's missing?" asked Lupa. "The one about plantations and history?"

Bailey stared at the brothers. "It's a library book. I have to return it."

"Why are you looking at us that way?" asked Archie.

"Are you accusing us?" asked Fendol. "That's pretty nasty of you, after all we've done to make you feel at home here."

"And knowing that you don't want your mother and our dad to get married, we've tried to keep you from doing things to stop them. Right, Fen?" said Archie.

Bailey's face burned as she continued to stare at them. Out of the corner of her eye, she was aware that Lupa was shocked.

"You know that's not true," Bailey said, trying to stay calm. "Where's my book?"

"Find it yourself," said Fen. "We have things to do." He and Archie smiled sweetly at Lupa and left the kitchen.

Lupa closed the lid on the cookie jar and said, "What's going on? You can tell me."

Bailey sat on a tall stool at the island in the center of the kitchen.

"I don't want more trouble," she said, burying her face in her hands.

"From Archie and Fendol?" asked Lupa.

Bailey nodded. "I don't know what to do," she said.

"I understand," said Lupa. She pulled up a stool next to Bailey. "I know all about them. I've known them since they were little and Andrew used to bring them here. They are full of pranks, sometimes mean ones. But they are also not 100 percent bad, although sometimes it seems that way." Lupa waited to see if Bailey would say anything. Bailey didn't.

"Their father should be more strict, but he's been busy with his research, and the book your mother wrote about him. He's been away a lot on book tours. He doesn't always know what Archie and Fendol are doing, and they often fool him by being nice when he's around. He doesn't notice when they're being bullies, and they always have excuses for what they do. They blame everything on other people, like now."

Bailey was really surprised to hear what Lupa was saying.

Lupa continued, "Marie told me and Chico some of what's been going on with them this week. It's not right and it will stop. I promise. We don't want you to have a bad experience during your visit, and they need to behave better in general."

"Please don't say anything to Mom or . . ."

"Bug Man?" Lupa asked with a soft laugh. "Don't worry. We don't want to do anything to upset them before the wedding."

Bailey lifted up her face, then gave Lupa a big hug.

17

Another trip planned

Lupa reminded Bailey of Sugar. She was wise and loving, and made good cookies, too. But how could Lupa, Marie and Chico make Fendol and Archie stop their mean pranks? And where was her book? She decided to look outside again.

From the front hall she could hear her mother and Andrew talking and laughing in the large living room. They were discussing plans for New Year's Eve, which was tomorrow, and then how early they would have to get up the following morning for the wedding.

Bug Man said, "I think we should have plenty of time to visit the volcano tomorrow. I'm sure Sugar and Bailey will find that fascinating."

Molly replied, "Perhaps you can take them, dear. I have an appointment to get my hair and nails done for the wedding."

"Well, then," said Andrew, "I'll ask them. It will be another chance for Bailey and my boys to get acquainted. It'll be quite a while before they see each other again."

Nooooo, screamed Bailey silently. *No. No. No! I don't care if I ever see them again.*

Before she could say anything, she felt Sugar's hands on her shoulders. Sugar turned Bailey toward her and said, "There you are. I've been wondering where you've been since we got back from town."

"Talking with Lupa. She's really nice," said Bailey. "She reminds me of you."

"Aw, you just want another invisible pony," said Sugar with her huge grandmother smile.

"And here's the rest of my new family," said Andrew, happily. "I've got a great idea for to-morrow while Molly gets fixed up, not that she needs to, for our wedding. I'll take you to Poás Volcáno. A volcano isn't something you see in the woods of Virginia. Poás is about an hour's drive. If we had more time I'd also take you to Arenal Volcáno, but that's a longer drive and we need to be back to celebrate the end of the old year."

"Fabulous," said Sugar.

"Wear good walking shoes and long pants," Bug Man suggested. "You might want a hat and hoodie and bring your cameras. The view is spectacular from the rim if the weather cooperates. We'll leave early, say about eight, so that we have plenty of time to walk up to the rim. It's best to see Poás in the morning."

Bailey stiffened. She tried to think of something else to do, but she really did want to see a volcano. If only Archie and Fendol wouldn't be along.

18

Poás Volcáno

Bug Man and the boys arrived early. He had a little gift for Bailey, a strap for her camera that would go around her neck. PURA VIDA, meaning, "the good life," was printed on it.

"Very Costa Rican," he said, fastening it to the camera. Now you won't have to hold your camera by the wrist strap while we walk around." He shoved his thick glasses up his nose, just like Sugar often did.

"Did you get your new glasses yet?" Bailey asked after she thanked him for the gift.

"'Fraid not. These are my old scratched pair, but they'll have to do until next week when the new ones are ready. Now, all aboard the Poásmobile."

Sugar sat up front in Dr. Andrew Snorge-Swinson's van, Bailey sat behind her grandmother, and the boys stepped through middle seats to sit in the way-back. Bailey knew that wasn't good. They would have a chance to poke her or yank her hair from behind. Or they would make nasty comments that only she would be able to hear.

While they were still on the back country roads, Andrew slowed to cross a creek and talked about the banana plantation, owned by a friend of Marie's. "Next time you come, we'll show you how bananas are harvested," he said.

Bailey was grateful that his sons were strangely silent. She listened as Sugar asked more about the volcano. Andrew said that Poás was active, but not erupting. That meant they should be able to see steam rising from the caldera deep inside the volcano's walls. "It looks like a pot about to boil," he said.

"Is it dangerous today?" asked Bailey.

"Not so much. Nothing to be concerned about." He continued, "I've seen Arenal erupting. It's exciting to hear it chuffing, and smoke comes out of the top, and red lava spills down the sides."

He didn't completely convince Bailey.

Sugar turned around, "Have you boys seen these places?"

"Yes, ma'am," Archie said politely.

"We like the Arenal volcano best, too," said Fendol. "Dad has told us all about the Pacific Ring of Fire."

"Have you studied the Ring of Fire in one of your library books, Bailey?" asked Archie, much too nicely.

Bailey tried to figure out how to answer without falling into a trap.

"As a matter of fact, yes," she said, loudly enough for her grandmother to hear. "Sugar has a wonderful bookstore and it has a section on Costa Rica."

"Oh," said Archie. "That's just terrific. You can tell us all about everything."

Bailey peered out the window. She wasn't going to say any more.

They reached the visitors center just as it opened. Bug Man said that it was only a short walk to the rim. The boys went on ahead, leaving Bailey with Sugar and Andrew. He stopped often to point out small bugs or birds that they might not have noticed otherwise. Bailey was astonished by the size of plant leaves, so big that some were taller than she was. "What are these called? They look like huge floppy umbrellas or elephant ears," she said.

Bug Man answered, "Aren't they wonderful! The shape is why they are often called the poor man's umbrella."

The sign above one large umbrella leaf warned in both English and Spanish that the volcano was active and visitors entered the park at their own risk. Bailey shivered with excitement.

The entrance sign and small umbrella plant.

Even though she had seen pictures in Sugar's books, Bailey was not prepared for the view of the volcano. It caught her breath. Poás was amazing. It was more than a mile across from rim to rim, with a bubbling blue-green lake with steam swirling out of it far below them. The volcano was just as Andrew had described.

And as he explained what they were looking at, he also pointed out the cloud forest, which was higher than the rain forest in the mountains. He said that when they came again, he would drive them there.

"Let me take a picture of you and Sugar with the volcano in the background," Bug Man said. Bailey and Sugar posed with big smiles.

The moment he was done, Bailey thought she heard someone yelling for help a lot farther along the path.

Bailey's pictures show steam rising out the lake in the crater's caldera.

Without waiting to tell Andrew or Sugar who were busy talking, Bailey ran in the direction of the shouting.

She saw Fendol lying on his side on the ground and Archie kneeling next to him. Fen was holding his bloody nose. Tears streamed down his cheeks.

"Get help!" said Archie. "Fen fell. Look at his face." He was frightened.

When Bailey hesitated, Archie begged, "I mean it. It's not a prank. Please help!"

"I'll be right back. But here's my jacket. Put it under his head."

"But it will get all bloody," said Archie.

"Doesn't matter," Bailey answered. She bent down and said to Fen, "Hang on. You'll be okay."

She ran back to where Bug Man and Sugar had been talking, but they weren't there now. Where could they have gone? She tried to ask tourists if they had seen her grandmother, but they lifted their hands. They didn't speak English. Bailey ran down to the visitors center. Sugar and Andrew weren't there either.

She checked Bug Man's van, then hurried back to the rim. Still no sign of Archie and Fen. Finally, far down the path, in the opposite direction from where the boys were waiting, Bailey saw Sugar using her binoculars to have a better view of the volcano park. Andrew was pointing out where to look.

Bailey ran up to them gasping for air. "Fen fell and he's hurt." She pointed in the boys direction.

Andrew dashed ahead of her on the path and reached the boys first. A crowd had gathered. One man offered to call for medical help. After taking a look at Fendol's injuries, Bug Man said he didn't think it was necessary.

"How'd this happen?" Bug Man asked. He sounded concerned and annoyed.

Archie looked ashamed but didn't answer. Fendol only moaned, "Ow! Ow!"

"I asked you what happened!" repeated Bug Man, now angrily. He crouched near Fendol while fixing his eyes on Archie.

"I saw it," said a tourist. "He climbed that tree, right by the sign that says to stay on the path."

"Then a branch bent and he tumbled down," said a woman with a baby in a stroller. "He landed face first. Serves him right." She clucked her tongue and shook her head. "Parents need to pay more attention to their kids," she added before walking off.

"What were you doing in the tree?" asked Andrew. "You know better. You are supposed to follow park rules for your own safety. How many times have I told you that?"

He wiped Fendol's nose with a clean handkerchief he had brought along for blowing his nose when his allergies bothered him.

His sons still didn't answer.

"I'm so sorry," Bug Man said to Bailey and Sugar. "Another day of your visit here and with more problems. I wanted to show you the best, but something keeps going wrong. I'm very sorry. I guess we'd better get his face taken care of."

With one last look at the volcano, Bailey and Sugar followed Bug Man and the boys to the van for the ride to the emergency clinic.

Archie continued to sit in the way-back. Bailey figured he still didn't want to answer his father's questions about what they had been doing before the accident.

19

Getting at the truth

The mountain clinic was filled with people who were sick or who had had accidents, so they had to wait an hour for a doctor to look at Fendol's face. He was lucky, the doctor said. Fen's nose was broken, he had chipped a front tooth, and would definitely have a black eye. He gave Fen an ice bag to hold on his face during the ride back to the hacienda.

His father helped Fen into one of the middle seats. Bailey offered to sit in the way-back so that Archie could be with his brother in the middle.

"Now, it's time for truth," said Andrew. What were you doing in the tree?"

"Nothing," said Fendol.

"Nonsense," said their father.

"Maybe we were having a better look at the volcano?" offered Fendol.

Yeah, sure, thought Bailey. *You could see it perfectly well from the path.*

"I *will* find out," said their father. "I have the feeling that you weren't up to anything good."

Looking out the window, Sugar said, "You know, sometimes people hide in a tree when they want to surprise someone who will be walking by. I'm not saying that this is what happened, but it's possible."

"I can't imagine that they would want to surprise or scare you, Sugar," said Andrew.

"No, it wasn't Sugar," Fendol blurted out.

"Don't say anything," Archie hissed to his brother.

"You told me to do it," Fendol hissed back. "Now I'm the one with a broken nose." He shifted uncomfortably in his seat. "I'm going to tell them."

Archie punched his arm.

Fendol said, "Okay, Dad. Yes, we climbed the little tree and we planned to scare . . . to scare Bailey. We figured she'd walk by herself in that direction. It was just a joke. A little prank, you know."

"Not nice," said Andrew gripping the steering wheel so hard that his knuckles were white.

"Well, I really am sorry, Dad," said Fendol, almost as if he had forgotten that Bailey was sitting right behind him. "She was really nice to me after I fell. She gave me her jacket. It's all messed up now from my bloody nose. I know we shouldn't have pranked her the last few days, but we didn't always know what could happen."

Bailey was completely surprised at his admission.

"So there have been other things that have been going on?" Bug Man asked. It sounded like his words were caught between his teeth, like a dog snarling while gripping bone.

Bailey wondered if he was expecting her to answer, but instead Fendol continued. "Uh, yes, Dad, but I think everything's okay now."

"Is it, Bailey?" asked Bug Man.

"I think so," she said, then leaned her head near the boys and said softly, "If the library book comes back."

"No worries," said Archie. "I'm sure you'll find it."

20

More e-mail

Bailey decided to check her e-mail before dressing for dinner. She figured she wouldn't have much time in the morning while they prepared for the wedding. The first was from Norma Jean, using their father's e-mail:

From: pjfish2005@yermail.net>
To: "Bailey"<baileyfish@gmail.com>
Sent: 4:25 p.m.
Subject: Hi

Dad said you went to the volcano today. So exciting! We are going to have a New Year's Eve party tonight and Sparrow is going to sleep over. Mom is even letting us stay up until midnight. I wish you were here with us. I can't believe that tomorrow is the wedding day. I looked on the Internet and saw that the weather is supposed to be really nice. No rain. It's still freezing here. Paulie has a cold and Sam and I might get it. We miss you soooo much.

What are Bug Man's sons like. Cute?

I hope you don't decide to stay in Costa Rica with your mom. Promise to come home.

NJ

Bailey sighed. No, she wasn't going to stay and what should she say about the boys? Nothing at the moment. She was glad that she had had a chance to see Costa Rica. It was more interesting and beautiful than she had imagined. And she was liking Bug Man better and better. He was so upset that so many of the plans had been spoiled, even though it wasn't his fault.

Tomorrow was the wedding. It was her mother's special day, and Bailey was the best girl. Her lilac dress was pressed and ready to wear. Even though she hadn't always felt this way, she really hoped that nothing would go wrong. No more broken windshields, no snakes falling from trees, no lost glasses, no ring in the trash, no missing book, no broken noses. No more pranks. No rain. She hit REPLY:

From: "Bailey"<baileyfish@gmail.com>
To: <pjfish2005@yermail.net>
Sent: 6:43 p.m.
Subject: Hi

I've got great pictures and will tell you everything when I get home with Sugar. Have to go to supper. Tell everyone hello. I miss them too.

Bailey

She hit SEND, and went downstairs. Instead of staying for supper and the family party, Andrew had taken the boys back to his house for a "talk."

Lupa told her that she was sure that there would be no problems with Archie and Fendol during the rest of Bailey's visit. "Once their father gets involved, he means business," she said.

"And by the way, Andrew asked me to give this back to you." She handed Bailey the book.

"How did he get that?" she asked, puzzled.

"Andrew said he found it on a porch chair, and was so interested in it that he was looking through it in the living room for a while," Lupa said.

"Hmm. Strange," said Bailey. She decided it didn't matter where the book had been or why. It was now returned and didn't look damaged.

Lupa had fixed a special dinner that began with ceviche and avocado. She explained that ceviche was fish that "cooked" in lime juice. Bailey tasted it and was surprised how good it was. And then there was fresh sea bass, and rice, and more of Lupa's coconut flan.

"I will miss cooking for all of you," Lupa said when dinner was finished.

"We'll just have to come back for another visit sometime," said Sugar.

"Any time," said Marie.

"They'll be visiting us, too," said Molly. "We're hoping that Bailey will come for the summer. What about that, girlfriend?"

Bailey didn't like being put on the spot in front of everyone. A lot could happen between now and then. However, her mother was waiting for an answer and she seemed so happy and hopeful.

Sugar looked at Bailey's face and said, "This has been a great trip. So much more to see the next time." She glanced at her watch. "It's later than I realized and I think I'll head to bed rather than stay up to welcome the new year. Tomorrow's a big day."

"Me, too," said Bailey.

Molly said, "Wait, before you go up, let's have a little mother-daughter time. Okay?"

"Sure," said Bailey.

She followed her mother out to the porch and they sat in the rockers near the door.

"Aren't the stars beautiful?" asked Molly. "When I'm so far away from you I often make wishes about us."

"Really? What kind of wishes?"

"Bailey wishes. Wishes that you know that I love you no matter what. That you know I think about you all the time no matter what. Wishes that I could be a better mother and be more in your life even though I have this wonderful job and have met a man whom I will marry tomorrow."

Then Molly sounded a little sad. "I know you don't want to move to Costa Rica to live with us, but I hope you'll want to visit a lot and get to know Andrew better."

Bailey rocked quietly for a moment. Even though she was afraid her voice would wobble she said, "You're a good mother, Mom. You sent me to live with Sugar while you were away and that's been okay. I miss you and I love you. And I'll always make Bailey and Mom wishes, too."

"C'mere," said Molly. "Let's sit in the double rocker so I can hold you close and we can wish on stars together."

Molly's arms wrapped around her daughter until Bailey's view of the stars was hidden by her mother's thick dark hair.

21

A visit with Sugar

Belleza's purring awoke Bailey at sunrise. January 1. A new year and the wedding day. Bailey slipped into her robe, grabbed her camera and hurried to the kitchen. Lupa was baking sweet bread, but she already had the platter of fruit ready for Bailey to take to the birds.

Bailey sat on the garden bench after refilling the bird feeder, and scattering pieces of melon, bananas, and pineapple on the lawn. Her camera was ready when the toucans appeared. Hummingbirds dashed to and from the

Another toucan visit.

flowers that had been planted to attract them. She heard the macaws and parrots in the trees. She would miss mornings like this when she was back home.

Bailey saw Sugar cross the yard slowly so as not to disturb the birds, then stop to watch the toucans. Once the toucans had returned to the trees, Sugar continued walking until she reached the bench.

"What a week it's been," said Sugar. "I'd love to see more of Costa Rica, but I'm ready to go home and get my bookstore open for business."

"Me, too," said Bailey.

"There's something I want you to know. I've been very proud of how you have handled things this week as the boys' pranks, if that's what they can be called, got worse. And you stood up, not only for yourself, but also for what was right. That takes courage."

"But how did you know?" Bailey asked, startled.

"I see things and I hear things," said Sugar. "That's what the Wild Women do." She patted Bailey's knee with her soft hand.

Sugar looked at Bailey and continued, "Andrew called a few minutes ago and said to expect a change in his sons' attitude today. They had a very long talk. Frankly, I'm glad he is getting more involved with their behavior and lives. I don't think we need to worry about what could go wrong at the wedding. At least not from them. Now let's have breakfast and get ready."

Bailey smiled. She felt much happier after talking to her grandmother. She knew that the day would be perfect after all.

22

Oh, no!

Lupa pulled up the long zipper in the back of Bailey's dress and clipped white and lavender orchids in her hair over her right ear.

"Just look at you," said Lupa. " You are as beautiful as your mother and my Marie."

Bailey stared at herself in the long mirror that Lupa had brought to her room. She'd rather be wearing her shorts and a T-shirt, but this outfit was okay, well, really okay for a wedding. She smiled at herself.

Sugar was wearing her deep-purple jacket dress with a matching orchid pinned near the jacket collar. "Don't we look fancy!" she said when Bailey came out of her room. "And wait until you see the bride. You'll be surprised!"

Molly was downstairs with Marie, who was checking her makeup and fussing with her hair. Molly's ankle-length, satiny red dress made her look like a model in a fashion magazine. Her long hair was tied to one side with an orange silk ribbon so that it fell forward over her left shoulder. She was wearing purple shoes, and a veil with white orchids fastened to the band like a crown of flowers.

"Wow," said Bailey, with a grin. "I thought you would wear white."

"Don't you love it? Red is so much fun," said Molly. She twirled so that her skirt flared out.

"Absolutely," said Sugar. "Love it!"

"We are fabulous!" exclaimed Molly. "The fabulous three. Come over here so that Enrico can take our picture."

Bailey hadn't noticed the photographer with his big black sack of equipment. "Can you take pictures with my camera, too?" she asked.

"Sure," he said.

She dashed upstairs and back down. He took a few more shots of all of them.

"Ready?" asked Marie. "It's time for us to walk to the wedding spot. First Bailey, then Sugar, then Molly. I will bring up the rear. We stop at the arbor covered with flowers. When the music starts, Bailey, you will walk slowly, like we practiced, up to the gazebo. Andrew and his best boys, will be waiting with you and the minister. And here's the ring for your mother to give to Andrew. Just wear it on a right-hand finger even though it's pretty big for you. When

Molly gives you the signal, step forward and give it to her."

"Gotcha," said Bailey.

Bailey slipped on the heavy gold ring. She was about to start down the path, when she turned and went back to her mother and gave her a light kiss on the cheek, so as not to mess up her makeup.

Molly's eyes were moist with happiness. "You are my best girl. Forever," she said. "Forever."

Bailey stopped at the flower-covered arbor, with its paper wedding bells rustling in the breeze. The chairs were filled with friends of Molly and Bug Man. It looked like everyone had cameras ready for pictures. Enrico had set up his tripod and cameras to the side of the gazebo and in other locations so that he could take photographs from many different angles.

Jorge and his friends were playing soft music for the guests to enjoy before the procession began. Bailey looked around and saw Andrew and his sons in suits, with a red bow tie for Andrew, and purple ones for Fendol and Archie. They were walking toward the flower-covered gazebo. Fen's puffy face was black and blue, which sort of matched his tie. There could be no hiding the accident at the volcano.

Bailey's special walking music—a tune called "Simple Gifts"—began. Marie motioned to Bailey to start. She stepped slowly as planned, carrying her bouquet of lavender and white orchids with both hands just under her chin. Bailey smiled as the guests took her picture. Suddenly her nose itched terribly. She held her breath, afraid that she was going to sneeze. It was getting worse, so she lifted her bouquet in front of her face for just a second while she scratched her nose.

That was close, she thought. Then her nose itched again worse than the first time. There was no holding back the sneeze but it came out like a squeak. *Phew.* But there was no stopping it. Bailey tried to stifle the sound of the next one, but that made it worse. This time the sneeze sounded like Donald Duck quacking. Her eyes were watering. For a moment she thought her dress might have a pocket with a tissue inside. Bailey dropped her right hand to her side to check, then remembered that of course there was no pocket in this fancy dress. Both hands were supposed to be holding the flowers. Her right hand returned to the bouquet. Bailey hoped that she would reach the gazebo without sneezing again. The boys were watching, and she knew that they might tease her later.

She was just halfway through the walk when the biggest sneeze of her life erupted like a volcano and she almost dropped the bouquet.

It seemed like forever before Bailey could finish her slow walk to her place to watch the rest of the procession. Her nose still itched. She hoped the sneezing was done.

She looked over at Fendol and Archie. Fen rolled his eyes and looked away.

Sugar was next, walking slowly and smiling at the guests, then the music changed to "Here Comes the Bride," and Molly, looking happier than Bailey could imagine, headed through the arbor for the gazebo. She had a dreamy expression as she glided slowly along the white carpet that the ushers had unrolled. Bailey saw how she and Andrew looked at each other with warm smiles, and she smiled, too.

There were prayers, more music, readings and then it was time for the ring ceremony. Archie handed Molly's gold band to his father to place on the bride's finger.

Then it was Molly's turn. She signaled to Bailey that she was ready for Andrew's wedding ring.

Uh-oh. Bailey looked at her fingers. *No ring? Oh, no, where is it?* Bailey stared at her feet and all around. No ring. Gone.

"It's gone," she mouthed.

"What?" Molly mouthed back. "The ring?" She looked surprised, then worried.

Molly whispered to Andrew, who whispered to the minister, who announced to everyone, "Folks, this has never happened before, at least not like this. I need you too look around where you are sitting to see if you can spot a man's gold ring. The groom's ring to be exact."

Hot tears filled Bailey's eyes. She was embarrassed and ashamed. Her one big responsibility at the ceremony was to hand her mother the ring but she had dropped it somewhere. Even though she didn't plan to, she was the one who was ruining her mother's wedding. She didn't know if she should help look for it or stand still or run back to her room.

Bailey watched the guests lift their chairs, and bend down to look on the grass. How would her mother and Andrew ever forgive her? Maybe they would think she did this on purpose. They were talking quietly together.

Then Andrew came over and said, "Hey, Bailey, your mom and I don't want you to worry and we certainly don't blame you. If the ring isn't found, we'll finish the ceremony anyway and keep looking later. It's just been one of those weeks when things have gone wrong, but, you know, it's really all right. Now, how about a hug from the best girl?"

"I'm so sorry. I didn't mean to drop it. Thanks," said Bailey, giving him a hug she really meant.

"We know," he said. "I'm a sneezer, myself. Sneezing happens."

Just then there was a shout from Chico. "I found it! I found it! She must have dropped it during her really big *estornundo*."

Bailey was puzzled. "Spanish for sneeze," whispered Andrew.

Chico rushed the ring to Molly and the wedding continued, with a wink for Bailey from Andrew.

"And I have photographed everything, including the sneezes and the finding of the ring," said Enrico. "Great memories for Dr. and Mrs. Andrew Snorge-Swinson."

"Wonderful," said Molly, "except that for now I'm still going to be called Molly Fish, so my daughter and I will have the same last name. She will always be my best girl."

22

A beautiful life

Bailey and Sugar were up early to finish packing. They wanted to see the toucans one last time, and then they would ride to the airport with Molly and Andrew for the eleven A.M. flight to Fort Lauderdale, then a second flight to Richmond. They were still full from the wedding feast that lasted until almost ten o'clock with lots of music and dancing. Even Bailey and Sugar had kicked off their shoes and danced to salsa music and did the Bunny Hop.

Belleza watched from a plump pillow on the bed as Bailey folded, well, stuffed her clothes in the suitcase. Her dress was rumpled and there was no need to pack it carefully now that the wedding was over. She wished she could take the warm Costa Rican weather back to Virginia. Her father's last e-mail said that although there were no new storms forecast, it would be very very cold. He said that the temperature at Lake Anna was 16 degrees and to dress warmly for when he would pick them up at the airport. She shivered at the thought of it. She wished her hoodie with LAKE ANNA printed on it hadn't been all bloodied up by Fendol's nosebleed. She knew that he couldn't help it, though, and everyone said she had done a kind thing when she tried to make him more comfortable after his fall.

Bailey sat next to Belleza and stroked her until she purred. "I'll miss you." The little cat blinked her solemn yellow eyes. "I'll come back. Maybe you'd like me to bring you a toy catnip mouse." She kissed her head.

"Ready?" called Sugar from the hall. "We have to leave very soon."

Bailey closed the maroon-colored carry-on, took one more look around her bedroom and wheeled the suitcase to the hall. Sugar was already halfway down the steps. Bailey followed, trying not to bump hers too hard on the polished wooden stairs.

"I need to say good-bye to Lupa," said Bailey. She found her in the kitchen fastening the lid on a shoe box. Bailey's name was on it.

"I'll miss you," said Bailey. "Maybe you can come see us sometime at the lake."

Lupa said, "You are so wonderful, Bailey. I wish you were staying longer. I was going to bring this to you. But *you* found me before *I* found you. They are cookies, special ones, from the wedding. There are plenty to share with your friends back home."

Bailey gave her a big hug, then hurried out to the yard where Chico and Marie were waiting by Andrew's car. It was hard to say goodbye to them without promising, especially when they insisted, that she would come back for a longer visit.

Fendol and Archie, with their hands behind their backs, were standing stiffly next to their father. Fendol's bruised face was turning new colors—purple, green and yellow. Bailey felt sorry for him even if he had brought it on himself.

Archie looked serious. He didn't smirk or make wisecracks about anything.

Dr. Snorge-Swinson cleared his throat and nudged his boys. Fendol stepped forward and pulled a bulky package from behind his back.

"We wanted you to have this," he said. "Something good to remember this place by, not by our pranks." He turned to look at his father.

Bailey was surprised and silent.

"And we're, uh, sorry," said Archie. "We didn't do everything you think we did, but we did and said some things that we shouldn't have, including about our mother. She didn't die. We just made that up. I don't know why we said that."

Bailey was astonished. They were apologizing. "Thanks," she said. She knew it was hard to apologize, and she had also done and thought some things she wasn't proud of.

"Here. This for you, and we paid for it ourselves," Fendol said quietly. "Open it."

Bailey tore off the yellow wrapping paper with butterflies printed on it, and smiled.

"So cool," she said as unfolded a new lime-green hooded jacket with COSTA RICA PURA VIDA stitched in bright blue letters on the front. She slipped it on. It fit perfectly.

"And here's one for Sugar, too," said Archie pulling a larger package from behind his back.

Sugar tore off the paper. Her jacket was identical to Bailey's, except for the size. "I love it," said Sugar. "It's very generous and thoughtful, and best of all, we will remember this moment always. Pura vida. It's a beautiful life, indeed."

Bailey waved until her hand hurt and the hacienda was out of sight. The goats were way out in the field when the car passed the fence but she snapped a picture to show Norma Jean and her friends anyway.

The drive to the airport seemed short, too short. There were no wandering cows or goats. Dirt back roads had quickly turned to busy paved highways filled with traffic and lined with shops and restaurants that were opening their doors for the lunch customers.

Andrew parked near the terminal and they headed inside.

Molly and Bug Man walked as far as they could before Bailey and Sugar would have to go by themselves through security.

"I really had fun," Bailey said to her mom.

"I knew you'd love Costa Rica," said Molly. "And we want you to come back soon, like this summer maybe? Even if it's just for a couple of weeks?"

"Okay, maybe," said Bailey. "We can do stuff together, if you're not too busy, and Lupa said she'd teach me how to make coconut flan."

"My girl," said Molly, hugging her. "I would take time off my job to be with you and we'll ride our invisible ponies to anywhere you want to go."

Bailey said, "I'd like that."

Bailey then turned to Bug Man, now her stepfather. She wasn't sure what to call him. She thought for a minute, then decided to ask him.

"Just Andrew," he replied. "Or, if you prefer, Bug Man. I really don't mind." His eyes twinkled at her through his thick glasses.

At first Bailey didn't know what to say, then she looked down at her new jacket.

"Pura vida," she said, smiling back. "Goodbye."

Discussion questions

1. Bailey is not thrilled that her mother is marrying Bug Man. What are some of her reasons for feeling that way?

2. Similarly, Fendol and Archie are not so happy their dad is marrying Molly. Are their reasons similar to Bailey's? Why or why not?

3. What are some things that surprised you about Costa Rica? What are some things Bailey liked about Costa Rica? What did Bailey learn about plantations in the United States vs. Costa Rica? Have you ever visited another country? If you could, what country would you like to visit and why?

4. On the river boat trip Bailey realizes that her soon-to-be stepbrothers are bullies. Can you name five things they do in the book that are really mean? Which do you think was the worst? Why?

5. What does Bailey do to get revenge when Fen and Archie trick her into ordering an octopus taco?

6. How might Marie know that Bailey is not happy about her mom's wedding? How does Marie know that the boys are up to no good? Did you think Bailey should have trusted Marie?

7. Grown-ups often say, "When you see something, say something?" In which situations does Bailey decide not to say something and why? What is the difference between "saying something" and just plain being a tattletale? Who are people you can trust with your story when someone is bullying you?

8. Sometimes it is a small kindness that changes someone's heart. Can you think of examples of kindness in the story (perhaps acts of Marie, Bug Man, Sugar, Bailey, Molly, Lupa, Chico) that changed a heart?

9. Do you think Bailey will go back to Costa Rica for the summer? Would you?

From Sugar's bookshelves

A Picture of Freedom, The Diary of Clotee a
   Slave Girl, Patricia C. McKissack
Eyes of the Calusa, Holly Moulder
From the Virginia Plantation to the Capitol,
   John Mercer Langston

Web sites

http:www.oberlin.edu/external?EOG/OYTT-images/JMLangston.html

http://www.powhatanmuseum.com/Powhatan_Honor_Roll.html

http://www.louisacountyhistoricalsociety.org/default.htm

https://pubs.usgs.gov/gip/dynamic/fire.html

http://www.tourism-costarica.com/

http://www.oberlin.edu/external/EOG/LangstonSpeeches/langston_menu.htm

Web sites were available at the time the book went to press.

Glossary

adobe: a heavy clay used to coat the outside of buildings.

autobiography: the story someone writes about his or her own life.

caldera: a large basin-shaped crater at the top of a volcano, formed by the collapse or explosion of the cone.

emancipate: to set free.

estuary: a place where the tide meets the river.

gazebo: a freestanding building with a roof and open sides.

hacienda: Spanish for a large estate.

orator: a person who is an outstanding public speaker.

Ring of Fire: a horseshoe-shaped string of 452 volcanoes and sites of seismic activity, or earthquakes, around the edges of the Pacific. Ocean.

Courage from Virginia's plantations

As Bailey learned about plantation life in Virginia, she was inspired by stories about two people who were born in Louisa County before the Civil War. One, John Mercer Langston, became a courageous American leader, and the other, Clara Garland, was known for doing what was right in her own community.

Material about John Mercer Langston comes primarily from his autobiography, *From the Plantation to the Capitol*.

Information for the section on Clara Garland has been adapted with permission from "The Garland Sisters & Garlandtown," an article by Kristin Hicks for the Louisa County Historical Society and from two talks by Elaine Taylor, director of the Louisa County Historical Society's Sargeant Museum. You can learn more about Clara by contacting the museum.

John Mercer Langston

On the sidewalk in front of the Louisa County, Virginia, courthouse stands an historical marker, which tells about John Mercer Langston, who became the first black congressman from Virginia after the Civil War.

There isn't enough room on the marker to provide the entire story of this amazing man's

This historic marker is located at the Louisa County, Virginia, courthouse.

life, starting with when he was born on a plantation called Poplar Grove located about three miles from the courthouse marker.

If you just want to know the highlights of his entire life, here are some important facts:

1. He was an orphan before age five.

2. He moved to Ohio, a free, not slave state, to live with the Gooch family, friends of his parents, who promised to care for and educate John.

3. His half-brother, William, kept him from moving with the Gooches to Missouri, a slave state, when he was about ten.

4. He entered Oberlin's prep school at age fourteen, then returned home and was asked to teach black students when he was sixteen. He returned to Oberlin to finish his education and received two degrees, his bachelor's and a master's in theology from the theology school.

5. Because of discrimination against black Americans, he couldn't attend law schools in the North or South, so with the help of friends, John studied law and passed the Ohio bar exam.

6. John was the first African American to win an election, although blacks were not allowed to vote, even in free states. He was accepted to practice law before the Supreme

Court. He was the friend of United States presidents and received important appointments from them, such as being named the ambassador to Haiti. He was appointed the inspector general for the Freedmen's Bureau after the Civil War. Among other things, the Freedmen's Bureau was created to help former slaves become educated and become established as free citizens.

7. He was the founder and first dean of the Howard University Law School.

8. He became the Commonwealth of Virginia's first African-American Congressman after Reconstruction.

Here are some cool stories from his autobiography

His father was Capt. Ralph Quarles, a wealthy white plantation owner in Louisa County, Virginia, who fought in the Revolutionary War. John's mother, Lucy Jane Langston, was a slave whom Ralph set free, along with their infant daughter, Maria. Lucy's background was mostly Native-American, with some black heritage. She was related to the Powhatans, the tribe of Pocahontas.

Besides Maria, Lucy had three other children, William, Harriet and Mary before John and his brothers were born.

Ralph and Lucy were forbidden by law to marry, but they lived together for many years and had three sons: Gideon Quarles, Charles Henry, and John Mercer (who was born in 1829). Ralph loved Lucy and the children, and personally educated the older boys, Gideon and Charles, starting when they were seven. The schooling began each day with their father at five A.M. before their chores. Ralph, Lucy, and their sons all knew the importance of being well educated.

Capt. Ralph Quarles probably built the tall part of the house in about 1778. Just behind the big house and connected to it by hallways is a second house, which had a kitchen below it. The homestead overlooks rolling fields where the crops were grown.

Above is the first-floor room of the second house. The door on the right leads to the front of the two connected buildings, and the door and stairs on the left lead to the second floor where this fireplace is found in a bedroom. The current owners, Jerl and Helene Purcell, are taking major steps to save this historic home of John Mercer Langston's father.

When John was four, both his parents died. His father was seventy, and his mother, fifty-four.

Ralph Quarles wanted to ensure that his sons received an excellent education and would inherit his money and property after his death. He also wanted to make sure that they would stay free so he made arrangements for John to move to Ohio and live with his friend, Col. William Gooch, his wife, Matilda and their three daughters.

Within two months of his mother's death, John remembers the sad farewells to the people he had been raised with and loved at the plantation, including an enslaved woman named "Lucky," who had tenderly cared for him when his parents were sick.

John, his brother, Gideon, and others left on wagons for the journey from Virginia to Ohio. Most had never been off the plantation. They crossed rugged mountains and streams and everyone was worried about little John and his health.

A week after they had left home in Louisa, the travelers pitched their tents at sundown, and took care of their horses. They were eating "cold food, with warm drinks of tea and coffee when a man on horseback, with saddlebags" appeared. Gideon greeted the man warmly as did everyone else.

The man picked up and hugged little John and told him he was the "very picture of his mother."

To John's great surprise, the man turned out to be his older half-brother William, whom he had never met. As they prepared to continue the journey, William, "as an expression of his love for him and to John's delight and satisfaction, arranged the stirrup-leathers of his saddle to fit his little legs and feet" so that he could ride William's horse.

John was fortunate to have his older brothers William, Gideon and Charles watching out for him during his early years. They made sure he was safe and had a good education.

John loved the Gooch family, who lived in a big stone house along the Ohio Canal in the Scioto Valley. The first thing Mrs. Gooch did when the little traveler arrived at his new home was to give him a bath and clean clothes. John says that she became his mother. He felt safe behind her apron. In fact, he was so much part of the family that he became known as Johnnie Gooch.

Like many children, he told a story that wasn't true. And he was caught.

John had been educated by one of the Gooch daughters until he was eight then the Gooches decided it was time for him to start public school. The school was located a mile and a half from the house. Mrs. Gooch was worried about him walking that distance given his "age, size and inexperience in self-management." So the family delayed sending him.

When he finally started a few months into the term, his teacher found him to be well-educated, but planned to give him extra attention in manners and behavior, if necessary.

Here's what John wrote about that first day. (In his autobiography he writes about himself in the third person.):

"With his little new dinner bucket, so clean and bright, full of nice things for his lunch, in one hand, and his books in the other, he moved off, in his neat, trim dress of roundabout and pants of Kentucky blue jeans, with stylish, fashionable cap and shoes, in cheerful spirits, to the experience awaiting him, which might make or destroy all his hopes."

He went on to say that school experiences "often handicap and ruin even promising children, boys and girls."

The school was in a Methodist church basement and the seats were made of "slabs, supported upon long round shaven legs at the center, without any rest of any sort for the back."

There were no desks. John said that for six hours every day the students had to sit on these uncomfortable benches. It was a new experience for a boy who was small for his age and used to comfortable seats.

He continued: "As he sat upon his seat, his little legs so short that his feet did not touch the floor, with no support for his back or any part of his person, his whole body became so filled with pain, acute and annoying, that no twisting or turning or stretching could or did give relief."

So, John tried to figure out what to do. He was "inexperienced in deception," he said, which meant he wasn't used to telling even little lies. But he came up with a plan. He decided to tell his teacher that he had to leave school every day at noon to go home to take care of the cows at two o'clock.

His plan worked for several days until his "father" saw him walking home when he should have been in school.

John didn't tell the truth at that moment either. He told Colonel Gooch that his teacher had let him come home.

Colonel Gooch went to school the next day, and had a talk with sweet Miss Annie Colburn, the teacher, assuring her that John was not needed at home with the cows, and that his business was to attend school.

After his father left, Miss Colburn asked John if he was sorry that he had told such stories.

John decided he'd better answer honestly this time, and he said, "No, madam."

As it turned out, she treated him so kindly and attempted to make him more comfortable that he "became earnest in his school work," and was an excellent student.

As history tells us, he was a brilliant scholar, learned several languages, including Latin, was a famous speaker and received two degrees from Oberlin College in Northern Ohio. John first received a bachelor's degree in 1849 and then a master's degree in theology in 1852. It was the first college in the nation to admit African-Americans (he was the fifth black student to graduate) and later women.

John had been encouraged to apply to Oberlin by his brothers and was accepted at Oberlin's preparatory department when he was just fourteen years old. After one year there, he was asked to teach black students near

Chillicothe. John wanted to return to college, but his half-brother William argued that he

A daguerreotype of John Mercer Langston from his Seminary class in 1853 at Oberlin. (Courtesy Oberlin College Archives.)

should take up a trade, asking John just what he would do with a college degree.

Fortunately, John listened to his own mind and the encouragement of Charles and others and he returned to his studies at Oberlin College.

John's career in law led him into politics and he became the first African-American in the nation to be elected to office as a town clerk in a community near Oberlin. He couldn't vote, nor could any other blacks or women, at the time.

He writes about his various encounters with racism during his life, such as not being allowed to attend law school, so he studied law with the help of abolitionist friends and passed the bar exams on his own.

Later in his life, after the Civil War and while efforts were being made to help freed slaves become educated and live independently for the first time in their lives, he was appointed to an important position.

In 1867, Gen. O. O. Howard asked John to serve as inspector general of the Freedmen's Bureau of Refugees, Freedmen and Abandoned lands, a job that the general said would be very difficult and would require oratorical skills. John would tour the postwar South and encourage freed slaves to seek educational opportunities and become a part of society.

He regularly spoke out against segregated places where blacks were not allowed to go with whites, including churches.

As inspector general, his district included Louisa County, Culpeper, Alexandria, Orange, Charlottesville, Gordonsville, Leesburg, Richmond and Petersburg.

Before he reached Louisa County, he had encountered trouble in Leesburg. The owner of a hotel would not let him in the dining room to eat with his friends, a group of generals who had invited him, because John was considered black. The hotel owner said his hotel would be burned if he let John in the dining room. John said that instead, he would eat in his room with the generals. A few days later when John and his friends returned to Leesburg, his friends weren't allowed in the hotel either because John was with them.

So with problems of prejudice and discrimination by some people toward blacks and their friends after the war, it wasn't surprising that John might encounter similar issues, even in his hometown. But the story of his visit to Louisa has a surprise ending.

John was greeted like a hero when he came back to Louisa Court House on June 15, 1867, for the first time since he had left at age four. He was there to inspect the schools and also visit the graves of his parents. And, it was in Louisa that he showed how his skills as a speaker could change hearts and minds.

John was welcomed by members of a club of black men, and then walked from the train station to the Louisa Hotel in the center of town.

As he entered the hotel he noticed a "large, fine looking, intelligent, influential man, apparently white, who seemed to be greatly angered about what was taking place."

That man was Gen. William F. Gordon Jr., a Louisa attorney, who was described as the "meanest rebel in the country. He's mad because we are having this meeting and you are to address us. He would break it up if he could, but thank God, he cannot," said the club president. His words worried John. But the crowd of more than 1,500 whites and blacks had come to hear the "Quarles boy," and "Lucy's son." And that's what John would do.

John was invited by the hotel owner to give his speech from the front porch of the Louisa Hotel. But standing nearby was General Gordon, "full of spite and anger."

In his introductory remarks, John talked at length about his life in Louisa, family, friends and career, the war, and his accomplishments. After about fifteen minutes, he noticed that General Gordon had moved to a chair on the porch with other prominent white listeners. The general fixed his eyes on John for the rest of the more than two-hour speech. When the speech was done, the crowd rushed forward with kind words and handshakes. Former slaves said, "God bless you. We are glad to see and hear you."

John was exhausted and told his friends he needed a brief rest. To his surprise, General Gordon was among those assisting him to his room. Then, to his greater amazement, John saw that the general was adjusting the pillows on his bed.

General Gordon apologized for the terrible things he had said about John. The general said, "Before you go to sleep, let me beg your pardon for the many blasphemous, vulgar expressions which I have made against you and against your coming here to address our people. I trust that you will forgive me. . . We are all proud of you. Your wonderful speech will do us incalculable service."

Later General Gordon asked John to speak to a white women's group at the Baptist Church. Although John was a worried that there might be trouble, he was assured that the general would be leading the meeting, John would be protected, and the women really wanted him to speak.

John wrote: "Certainly Louisa Court House has never witnessed a more beautiful, orderly, and enthusiastic female assembly . . . The Beautiful Virginia daughters of Louisa County gave him a royal, memorable reception" when he spoke about "the duty of American woman in this hour of our reconstruction."

And one further surprise, General Gordon invited John to join him for breakfast the following morning.

Although his talks were persuasive and important, because of racial prejudice, he still had enemies who didn't want him to be elected as the first African-American congressman after Reconstruction. They used dirty tricks and election fraud to keep him out of office.

He finally was declared the winner, when the fraud was proven, but by then seven months had gone by of his two-year term.

John only served one term. His enemies were still against him in Virginia, so he refused to run again. He continued, however, to be involved in politics and public speaking. He wrote his book *From the Virginia Plantation to the National Capitol*, which was published in 1894. In retirement, he continued to be proud of his children and grandchildren.

This great American, John Mercer Langston, died at home in Washington, D.C., on November 15, 1897.

Clara Garland

Another person from Louisa County, who showed courage at about the same time as John Mercer Langston was Clara Garland. Even though she wasn't famous, her story is a reminder that it's important to stand up for what is right in your community just because it is the right thing to do.

As historian Elaine Taylor tells us, "What makes Clara unusual is that she favored emancipation long before and after the war and was one of the most outspoken women to see that justice was done to the freedmen then in her care."

We don't know what Clara looked like. Some of what we know about her comes from her letters and entries in other people's diaries.

Clara and her three sisters were unmarried and ran the business of two plantations at a time when married women were not allowed to vote or own property. Clara and her sisters,

Ann, Amanda, and Rebecca, knew how to run the household, including taking care of the family, and the many slaves who lived on the plantation. The sisters directed all the work needed to care for farm animals and crops. Even though Clara and her sisters inherited seventy slaves, and owned 750 acres, they did not like slavery. Clara and her sisters were unlike many other plantation owners. They believed in education, freedom and justice both before and after the Civil War.

After Ann, the oldest, had to be hospitalized in 1849 for the rest of her life, Clara had to take over as the "eldest" in the household. That meant she was in charge of the plantation business and the family's social activities. These activities could mean welcoming travelers to stay with them, going to church or parties or having a special dinner. A former schoolmaster at Apple Grove wrote in his diary that on May 21, 1851, "I staid last night at the house of my very kind friends, the Misses Garland, and, among other things, was treated at supper to a dish of fine strawberries and excellent milk."

The sisters and their guests would have talked about what was going on in the world and in their community. As a woman with strong opinions Clara would have mentioned her views on education and slavery and had lively discussions with her guests.

Before the Civil War ended and slaves were freed, they didn't have any say over what happened to their husbands or wives or children. Slave families were often split up and sold to owners in other states. After the Civil War, former slaves were still at risk, sometimes because of what their own relatives did to them.

Clara Garland, at age sixty-five, decided to fight to help a former slave reunite with their families. She helped a former slave, Patrick Graves, who later became the first pastor of the Laurel Hill Baptist Church, to have his wife and children returned to him.

Graves also received ten acres of land when Clara L. Garland deeded land to her former slaves.

Three months later, Clara campaigned for the return of children taken from another former slave, Nancy "Nannie" Minor. In April 1866, Clara wrote to the commanding officer of the Freedmen's Bureau in Louisa County (remember that John Mercer Langston was inspector general for the Freedmen's Bureau) because Nancy's husband Watson had taken their children and had married someone else.

What he did next was terrible. He "bound out" the little boys, ages seven and ten. That means, he took his boys and essentially gave them away to someone else to work as servants until they became adults. Even though the children and their mother, Nancy, were freed after the war, the boys were now treated like slaves, and Clara Garland was upset. She had known these children while they were growing up and was worried about what was happening to them. Nancy wanted her children back and Clara agreed to help her.

Clara Garland wrote letters to the Freedmen's Bureau, and by June 3, 1867, both children were returned to their happy mother.

The Mt. Garland Baptist Church in Louisa County was established in 1866 with the help of the Garland sisters, who donated an acre of land to the project. Mt. Garland School, located adjacent to the church, came about later due to efforts of the church.

Acknowledgments

I have so appreciated the encouragement of readers, bookstores, and friends through the years as the Bailey Fish Adventures progressed to this one. Special thanks to my husband, Jim; Abigail Grotke; Nancy Miller (for discussion questions and photographs of leaf-cutter ants; Elaine Taylor, executive director of the Sargeant Museum of the Louisa County Historical Society; historical researcher Kristin Hicks; Ken Grossi, Oberlin College archivist; Helene Purcell and her husband Jerl, for a tour of Poplar Grove, the home of Ralph Quarles (father of John Mercer Langston); Mary-Frances Hoh; Pamela Gastineau; Shanna Hart; Julie Franklin, and as always, inspiration for the entire series from Amberlyn.

As for the photographs, some are mine, others come from sources, such as Nancy Miller (leaf-cutter ants on logs, page 57); Donna Barron (arbor, page 30), plus photos released to the public domain, including the close-up of the leaf-cutter ant on, page 58; owl butterfly on the right, page 58; crocodiles on pages 67 and 68, and the toucan on page 52.

About the author

 Linda Salisbury draws her inspiration for the Bailey Fish Adventure series from her experiences in Florida and Virginia, and as a mother, grandmother, mentor, and foster mother. She's a musician and enjoys boating and traveling. She has visited Costa Rica several times. She was born in Oberlin, Ohio, and is a graduate of Oberlin College, with a bachelor of arts degree in English.

Her books have won many awards, including from the Moonbeam Children's Book Awards, Eric Hoffer book awards, *Foreword* magazine, Florida Publisher's Association, and Virginia Press Women's Association.

In 2013, *The Ghost of the Chicken Coop Theater* was selected by Indiana Public Radio's *StoryBoard* program to be read aloud.

Besides *What Could Go Wrong?*, the Bailey Fish Adventure series includes *The Wild Women of Lake Anna; No Sisters Sisters Club; The Thief at Keswick Inn; The Mysterious Jamestown Suitcase; Ghost of the Chicken Coop Theater; Trouble in Contrary Woods; Captain Calliope and the Great Goateenies; Treasure in Sugar's Book Barn; Earthquake Surprise;* and *Snooper Dude's Secret.*

The series have fictional characters, but each book contains a nonfiction element, such as gold mining, Jack Jouett's ride, Civil War history, the story of Henry Box Brown, Jamestown history, and information on presidents, such as George Washington and Thomas Jefferson, or circus history.

She's also the author of *Mudd Saves the Earth: Booger Glue, Cow Diapers and Other Good Ideas,* a humorous environmental book for ages seven and up.

She's also the author of several books for adult readers, including, *But You Don't Look Funny,* and *Mother's: a novel of hoarding, friending and mischief.*

She lives at Lake Anna, Virginia, with her husband, Jim, and busy, creative cats.